LADDER TO
THE SKY

LADDER TO THE SKY

Ruth Forbes Chandler

ILLUSTRATED BY HARPER JOHNSON

Abelard-Schuman
London   New York   Toronto

London	*New York*	*Toronto*
Abelard-Schuman	Abelard-Schuman	Abelard-Schuman
Limited	Limited	Canada Limited
8 King St. WC2	6 West 57th St.	896 Queen St. W.

Printed in the United States of America

TO *George Lawrence Chandler*

CONTENTS

LADDER TO THE SKY

CHAPTER ONE

SCHOOL

It was a yellow slip of paper about three inches by five, but to Chip Wood it was poison. The minute Mr. Stringer laid it on his desk, Chip stuck it between the pages of his English book. If looks could kill, Stringer would have been a dead duck.

Chip had had deficiency slips before, but this time it was different. These last two months he had worked. Like an old monk in a cell he'd kept at it, plugging away night after night to bring that English mark up. If he ever hoped to get to college he must get passing grades.

And there was another reason: his sister Carol. She was two years younger than Chip but only one year behind him in school. Her report cards were decorated with a monotonous pattern of A's. If he had to repeat

11

and be in a class with her. . . . His eyes grew thoughtful and he chewed the knuckle on his thumb. No sir. He wouldn't do it. He'd quit school first.

But he couldn't quit. A good education was more necessary for him than for most boys because he was colored, and if he was going to amount to anything he would have to prove he had a good brain and a good character. All his life long his father and mother had kept telling him that, and Chip knew it was true. It was the reason behind his working so hard on those English assignments. He had made up his mind never to be stuck with another deficiency slip. And here was old Stringer handing him one again.

He sighed a deep whistling sigh as he piled his books on his desk and pushed his long legs into the aisle ready to beat the bell. Before it stopped buzzing he was out the door, falling into step beside his tow-headed pal, Butch Swanson.

"What's the matter?" Butch asked. "Did Stringer flunk you again?"

"He did." They elbowed their way down the corridor. "What gets me is to fail English. I get good marks in everything else. But English! Everybody knows English from the time they can talk. And me, I have to flunk it."

"That stuff Stringer hands out isn't English," Butch commented sympathetically.

"You said it. Participial phrases, infinitives. What good does it do anybody to know stuff like that?"

"Search me."

They left the building together, in perfect agreement

as usual, and made their way to the baseball diamond where boys were assembling for a practice game.

"I can't stay very long. I've got to spade up a place so we can transplant our iris," Chip explained as they reached the field. "It'll be easier to show my dad this yellow ticket if I get my work done first."

It wasn't that his father would find fault. He would be disappointed, and that was harder to take. Chip and his father understood each other. From the time he was a baby, the boy had been "a chip of the old block" and the early nickname had stuck. They looked alike, with broad shoulders and long slim bodies, round faces, and wide smiles that showed beautiful white teeth.

They were alike inside, too, friendly and generous, believing in the fairness and good will of the people they met. Both had hot, quick tempers which they tried hard to control, the father succeeding more often than the boy. They were inclined to be easy going if it was possible, but they could hang on like bulldogs when they set their hearts on anything. And Chip had set his heart on passing English. It rankled that he had failed.

Butch roused him from his unhappy thoughts. "Uh oh, Freddy Greer's out there again." He bobbed his head towards a redheaded senior who was barking orders at the younger boys.

"What is this, Friday the thirteenth?" Chip asked. "It's my unlucky day all right. Butch, I'm going to talk to him." He laid his books on the players' bench. "I'm going to tell him..."

"No. You'd better let me do the talking," Butch said

slowly. "He's mean to everybody, but he's out to get your goat. You don't want any more trouble with him."

"Okay. I suppose you're right. But give it to him straight. Don't be afraid. I'll go with you, but I'll keep still."

"Hi, Freddy," Butch began. Freddy turned his back and stooped to pick up a ball. "Freddy," Butch tried again, "last year I pitched and Chip was catcher on our team and we came in second in the Little League."

"So what?" Freddy slammed the ball across the field and waited for the return throw. "Too high," he yelled and threw again. "And get that fool dog off the place," he ordered, as a small brown dog trotted across the diamond. Three boys raced after it while Butch and Chip looked at each other. Freddy made everybody step, all right. It burned Chip up.

Without waiting for Butch to get the courage to try again, Chip stepped in front of Freddy. "Look," he said, "we sat on the bench all yesterday afternoon, and you didn't give us one chance to play. I've got work to do. If I can't play, I'm going home."

Freddy gave him a withering glance. "Go on. What's stopping you?"

Chip bit his lip and counted ten. "We've got as much right to play as anybody else. Mr. Kelley told us to try out. Yesterday you gave some fellows two and three chances. . ."

Freddy turned on him. "Are you telling me how to run things? I'm boss until Kelley gets here. Make up your mind. Do you want to stay, or do you want to go home and plant pansies?"

The muscles in Chip's arms twitched with the effort it took to keep them at his side. "I want to play ball," he said, his eyes never leaving Freddy's face. "What else I do is my business."

"Get over on the bench, then. You, too, Swede. Wait your turn like everybody else." His lips curled in a snarl as the dog came back, nose close to ground, sniffing around second base for some familiar scent. Freddy hurled the ball at it, missing it by an inch, and the pup, its tail between its legs, ran yipping into the street.

A shiver of pain ran through Chip's body. He had promised his father not to fight, not to get into trouble, but it seemed as though something inside his head would burst with the pressure of his anger. He couldn't hold back the words, "Sure. Hit a little dog. That shows the kind you are."

"Dry up. If I'd wanted to hit it, I would have hit it. Get over there and sit down, or go on home." Freddy walked toward the home plate. "You fellows I chose, line up; get to your places. The rest of you watch and listen to me. All ready. Play ball."

Chip and Butch joined the other seventh graders and roosted on the bench for an hour. Then Mr. Kelley came, and they got their turn. In his one chance at bat, Chip struck out, and in the next half at first base, he muffed a fly. Butch was just as bad. It was as though Freddy had put a jinx on them.

"I wish I'd gone home and not wasted the whole afternoon," Chip said when it was over.

"Me, too," Butch agreed. "Freddy Greer may know baseball but he's no good as manager or coach. He wants everybody to know he's the big shot, and you, you're nothing."

"He's always been like that. He's the meanest kid in the State of Massachusetts."

With both the late hour and the deficiency slip to weigh him down, Chip's feet dragged as he turned into King Street. It was a short, friendly little street, where everybody knew everybody else. If there were hedges between the houses they were so low that children and their dogs could jump them. The yards were well cared for. Already crocuses and scillas were blossoming in sheltered corners.

The Woods' house was much like the others, but their garden was the prettiest one on the street. Chip's father had bought an adjoining lot, where he raised flowers to sell. It was a hobby that was fast becoming a profitable business. In Chip's opinion, gardening was an awfully hard way to earn money, but he helped because his father needed him.

"Be seeing you," Butch said, turning at the walk that led to his back door.

"Sure thing." Chip went on to the house across the street, where the kitchen smelled of gingerbread, and a tall dark woman in a crisp blue gingham dress looked at him with disapproval.

"I thought you were coming home early tonight to help your father," she said.

"I was, but..."

"*But*," she repeated. "There's always a *but* while your father works himself blind in that office, and then comes home to work until dark in the garden. You say you'll help. Oh yes, you'll come straight home from school. You'll paint the blinds; you'll take care of the garbage and put out the trash barrel; you'll spade up the garden. But you never do. Here." She cut off a generous chunk of gingerbread and poured a glass of milk. "Get something in your stomach, change your clothes and get to work."

"I'll help Dad all day tomorrow," Chip promised with his mouth full. He set the empty glass in the sink, turned on the water and grinned at his mother. "Good gingerbread, Mom."

"Get going," she said, the dimple that made her look so young denting her cheek. "Hurry up, before I 'good-gingerbread,' you!"

CHAPTER TWO

FAMILY

For nearly an hour Chip worked with spade and fork, breaking up heavy clumps of rich brown earth and shaking them apart. The smell of spring was in the air, and a fat robin followed him, looking for worms. When their car turned into the drive, Chip went at once to meet his father, determined to tell about the English failure and get it over. His father looked so tired as he stepped out and straightened his shoulders that Chip wished more than ever that he had good news instead of bad.

"I'm glad to get home," Mr. Wood said, taking off his glasses and squeezing his eyes shut and opening them again. "For four solid hours I've sorted punched cards and run them through the tabulator. What a way to make a living!"

"Why did you have to do cards?"

"Two girls out, and their work piling up. I can't do

18

mine until I get their figures, and the top brass are hollering for the reports. Lucky the old man can do everybody's job." He reached into the back seat for a bulging briefcase.

"I'll help you with your work, Dad," Chip said. "I'll read off the figures for you. But you aren't an old man." He felt a twinge of doubt, for his father looked old as he stood there.

"I feel as though I were a hundred and ten. I certainly hope I can quit this rat race before my eyes give out entirely."

"Why don't you, Dad? Why don't you buy that farm we saw in Redfield, the one on the hill with the big barn? If you had a flower farm you could work outdoors. You wouldn't be looking at figures all day long."

"I'd like to have that place. It's a good buy." He set his briefcase down and his face brightened. "I went to see the owner today."

"You did? Is it all right? Would he sell to us?"

"Yes. He had no objections. His name is Collins, and he seems to be a fine old gentleman. He told me he had lived there all his life. His wife died two years ago, and after that he was pretty lonely. He's over eighty. His son finally persuaded him to sell off his things and go and live with them."

"They live in Courtney?"

"Yes. But he misses the old place. He talked with me a long time, my whole lunch hour in fact. He says another party is looking at it, and they've been back three times, but he seems to want us to buy it. He was very nice.

He told me there are two other colored families in the town and they get along all right with everybody."

"How much does he want?"

"Eight thousand. We would do the buying through his agent, a man who lives in Redfield, name of Tower. Mr. Collins says there are ten acres, five cleared. The house has electricity but no plumbing, no furnace. It probably needs repairs. Old houses always do."

"We could fix it up ourselves after we moved in."

"I'm afraid your mother wouldn't like waiting for that.

"I wouldn't mind. I guess it's you and me against Mom and the girls."

"No. We don't take sides in this family. When we move, it will be because everybody wants to."

"Then we'll never move." Chip wished he hadn't said it as he watched his father go slowly up the stairs.

He went back to his digging, his head full of troubled thoughts. His mother wouldn't want to leave King Street. She was proud of living there, in a nice house in a nice part of town, and having the other women drop in for a morning chat, a cup of coffee, and some of her crisp doughnuts.

How often, when he was little, she had told Chip he must be polite, he must not fight or quarrel because people would be watching to see how he behaved. As he grew older and understood why she had said it, he had tried to keep out of trouble. It hadn't been easy. Most of the people were nice, but not all. Freddy Greer's family had lived there once, several years ago. Chip scowled as he thought of them.

Leaning on his spade, he tried to think it through. Life was pretty complicated, different people wanting different things, or not knowing what they wanted. What did he want? What did he really want?

If they bought the Redfield farm and raised flowers as a business and had a greenhouse, which was what his father wanted, what would it mean to Chip? His father wanted him to go to college, but what did he want himself? The flunk slip darkened his thoughts. Did he want to study for years and years? He looked at the swelling buds on the maple tree and the fluffy white clouds in the sky, and he knew the answer. He'd like to quit school now and work outdoors all the time. It would be a lot easier.

"Oh, look at the scarecrow! For a minute I thought it was alive." The words and the giggle that followed brought him back to earth. He knew without looking that it was his sister Carol and her friend Joanie. They were always together. They went to the movies and the library, and they studied fashion magazines, and they talked about school and clothes and boys all the time. When they got home, they called each other on the phone and talked some more.

"What are you doing?" Joanie asked, tossing her black braids and rolling her big brown eyes at Chip.

"Digging clams."

That brought another burst of giggles from Joanie, for while Carol was so quiet and ladylike that she said thank-you and pardon-me-please whether she needed to or not, Joanie was a silly thing, a rowdy little clown.

Chip decidedly was not interested in girls. But he kind of liked Joanie.

Joanie's family were the only other colored people on the street. It was when they moved in that Freddy Greer's family moved out because, they said, the place was getting cloudy. Joanie's father was a postman. Her big sister was a nurse. Her brother, whom Chip admired greatly, was stationed at the Naval Air Base at Quonsett. Their mother and Chip's mother were very good friends, and Joanie just about lived at Chip's house. It would break Carol's heart to move away and leave her. Chip's thoughts were back where he started as he tackled his job again. Yes sir, life was complicated.

He had worked another half hour, long enough to get a blister on his hand, when a clump of earth struck him between the shoulders and loose dirt sifted down his neck. At the same time came the shrill cry, "Supper's ready."

Turning, he saw his little sister Dolly wallowing through the soft earth, giggling, and looking back over her shoulder to see if he was chasing her.

"Wait till I catch you," he shouted. "I'll pick you up by your pigtails, and I'll turn you upside down, and I'll plant you, like a . . . like a . . ."

"You'll have to catch me, first," she called back, dancing up and down on the path.

Chip took giant strides through the field holding his fork as though it were a bayonet. "Here I come. Look out, you little rascal." He threw his tools in the direction of the shed and raced after her.

"You can't catch me. You can't catch a flea," she squealed, starting to run.

He caught her and boosted her onto his shoulders where she sat happily, one short dungaree-clad leg on either side of his neck, while she held firmly to his hair with both hands.

"Run, run!" she cried, banging his head to speed him up.

He ran to the yard and dumped her on the grass, then went into the house to wash up. He knew by the good smell that it was potroast for supper, and he wasted little time at the sink. After his half hour's rest, Chip's father felt like himself again, and the mealtime was pleasant as always, with everybody talking and laughing. Chip forgot for the moment that life was complicated, and that there was a small yellow slip in his English book.

Carol brought his troubles back. "They gave out warning slips in my room today," she said. "Nearly half the class got one, but I didn't."

"Why do you have to talk about school all the time? Why can't you forget it once in a while?" Chip growled.

"Why shouldn't I talk about school if I want to? And why do you have to scowl like an old grizzly bear?"

"That's enough," her father said. "What's the matter, Chip?"

"Stringer flunked me again. After the way I studied, too."

They were sympathetic and it was good to talk, to tell how hard he had studied, and to mimic Stringer, the old crab. From that, Chip went on to the baseball practice and Freddy Greer.

"You know, Dad," he concluded, "if we do buy a farm, I'm going to chuck school."

"I thought you were going to college and be a doctor," Carol interrupted.

"No. He's going to be a scientist and go to the moon on a great big rocket ship, aren't you, Chip?" Dolly asked, shaking her spoon at him.

"Oh, that was last year. I don't want to go to college. It takes too long. I've decided it's more practical to learn the work I'm going to do by doing it. If we buy a farm, I can experiment and learn all there is to know about soil chemistry." Chip liked the sound of that. Soil chemistry. It seemed so far removed from actual work with spade or hoe. He expounded the advantages of leaving school at once so earnestly, and became so wrapped up in his subject, that he ate his gingerbread with its crown of whipped cream without knowing it.

"There's nothing wrong with your English when it comes to an argument," his father said with a smile. "No matter where we live, you'll finish high school, so don't get any funny ideas about that. But I should like to ride out to Redfield tomorrow and take a look at that farm we were talking about. What do you say, Mother?"

She hesitated a minute, then answered soothingly, "Yes, dear, let's go. It can't do any harm to look."

CHAPTER THREE

FARM

Chip woke that April morning with a pleasant sense of expectancy. It felt like a good day for adventure. The last dirty patches of snow were melting and the grass at their edges was turning green. Leaf buds were swelling, daffodils were pushing up to the sunlight. All outdoors smelled of spring and growing things. Chip breathed it in deeply, filled with excitement. Maybe today the Woods would buy a farm.

At breakfast he asked his father about the agent. "Have you called him yet to get an appointment? Will he let us go inside the house and barn?"

"I called him last evening. He'll meet us at three o'clock, and this time we'll see everything."

"May Joanie go with us?" Carol asked, as she drowned her pancakes in maple syrup.

"No. This is a family affair."

25

Chip looked at her in disgust. "What do you want Joanie for?" he asked. "Mom, look at the maple syrup. She can't eat bread or potatoes because it makes her fat, but if it's something sweet she eats enough for the whole family."

"Eat your breakfast," his mother ordered, coming in with more pancakes, and the "no fooling" look on her face. She wasn't happy, Chip could tell. But she'd like the farm when she got settled on that beautiful hillside. This morning he was sure of it.

He whistled as he went to the plot where thousands of pansy plants were budding under their winter cover. They would have to be transplanted; the double English violets in the cold frame, too. It would be a lot of work to move a garden, but Chip wished he could begin that very minute.

He saw his father walking toward him. "Chip," he said, "come into the tool shed a minute. I want to talk to you." He sat down on a battered old chair, and Chip leaned against the potting bench.

"Before we see the agent, I want to be sure you understand what it will mean if I give up my job in the office," he said slowly. "You'll have to work. Really work. No more of this having to be told half a dozen times, or leaving every time you want to play ball. We'll be up against it for the next few years, everything going out and nothing much coming in."

"I'll work, Dad. I want the farm as much as you do, and I know it's the best thing for you." Chip felt a tightening in his throat as he remembered the day Dr.

Graham had come to look at Dolly's sore throat and had looked at her father instead.

"Charles," he'd said, "you're the one who needs the doctor. You'll have everything in the book if you don't get out of that blankety-blank office. You're a square peg in a round hole and you'll never be any different. Why don't you quit and do something you can put your heart into?"

His father explained that good office jobs were hard to get, and that he couldn't leave work that paid well for the uncertainty of something he might enjoy more. Then they'd gone up to see Dolly, but Chip had never forgotten that warning, or the stab of fear he had felt.

"Maybe it would be the best thing for me," his father said slowly, holding a broken flower pot in his hands and fitting the two pieces together carefully, "but it's you I'm thinking about. You'll finish high school, but if you want to go to college you'll have to get scholarships and work your way through. I don't know whether you've got it in you to do it. It will take a long time. And it may be that you'll have to stay on the farm and work so that we won't lose everything we put into the place. If I can't afford to hire help, you'll have to work there, for little or nothing. It's your future I'm worrying about."

"Well, stop worrying. It doesn't bother me at all."

"That's the trouble. Perhaps you're too young to realize what it means." He laid the flower pot down and stepped out into the sunlight. Following, Chip reached down and picked a dandelion that was opening its big

golden blossom on a one-inch stem, doing its best, like
a Cub Scout. That's all there is to it, Chip thought, do
your best; everything will turn out all right. He shook
off the serious mood caused by his father's words and
looked up with a smile. "I bet in a year or two we'll be
making more money than you earn now. You just wait
and see. Everything's going to be all right."

"I wish I could be as sure as you are. I wish I could
see five years ahead, or even two." He picked up the
spade and fork Chip had left on the ground all night,
shook his head, and went back into the tool house to
hang them up.

The Woods were at the farm long before the appointed
time. It was on Stonybrook Lane, a narrow dirt road,
just off the main highway that went over Quaker Hill.
The view of Redfield and the hills and woods beyond
was breath-taking that spring day. What would it be like,
Chip wondered, glistening with snow in winter, or bright
with autumn colors!

The house was a small red cottage with white blinds
and white chimneys, a sunny bay window on one side,
and a wide porch across the back. The barn was very
large. A brook ran from under the roadway, flooding out
into a tangle of bushes.

Mr. Wood opened the car doors. "Everybody out," he
said.

"May we look for baby frogs?" Carol asked.

"Yes, but be careful of your clothes. Don't get dirty,"
their mother warned.

Assuring her they wouldn't, the girls ran to the mea-

dow to find a good place to see the brook. Chip and his father walked across the fields, talking about gardens and where a greenhouse could go, while Mrs. Wood peered through the windows at the empty rooms. When the agent's car arrived it drew them together like a magnet. Mr. Wood bowed and introduced his family.

The name, Tower, suited the agent for he was tall, like a grand-daddy-long-legs in immaculately creased trousers. He greeted them politely, and they followed him into the house.

"I understand you have already met Mr. Collins," he said.

"Yes," Chip's father answered. "Since we are colored, I thought it would be best to see the owner before we took any of your time."

Chip was proud of his father at that moment. He couldn't put his feelings into words, but he held his head a little higher because of the dignity and forthrightness of his father's reply. How could Mr. Collins, or Mr. Tower, or anybody refuse to sell to him?

Chip looked at his family while the two men talked,

trying to see them through Mr. Tower's eyes. His
father and mother were neatly dressed, and had pleasant
intelligent faces. He wasn't much to look at himself, but
he was neat and clean, and his sisters were scrubbed
within an inch of their lives, and all dressed up in their
Easter hats and coats. They looked all right to Chip.

He wandered through the four downstairs rooms—living room, dining room, big bedroom, kitchen—and came
back to listen to what Mr. Tower was saying: "You may
want to whiten ceilings and paint and paper some of
the rooms, but the place is sound. It's a remarkable
bargain."

Chip saw his mother looking at the black iron stove,
the pump, and the rusty sink, with a fierce, cold look
in her eyes, and he opened the back door and went out.

He wished he could get into the barn. It was a fine
big building with a high cupola, and on it a golden ball,
and high above that, shining against the blue sky, was
a clipper ship with tall masts and one sail set to catch
the slightest breeze. Was the sail metal, he wondered,
and had Mr. Collins made it? Had he been a sailor,
perhaps, when he was young?

Chip saw the others coming from the house, Dolly
ahead to be first with the news. "We can each have a
room, and I chose the one with pink paper. And at
Christmas we can have Grandma and Grandpa and Aunt
Molly and all the children. Mama said so."

"You like this place?"

"I do. I do. I do." She bounced up and down, pigtails
flying, to prove how much she liked it.

Mr. Tower opened the padlock and rolled back the wide barn door. They all went in. They walked around on the wide rough boards looking at empty stalls and grain bins. There was a rickety ladder to the mow, and Dolly was halfway up before her father picked her off and set her on the floor. When the others left, Chip stayed behind. He'd never been in such a big barn before, and he wanted to look around.

On the right of the big door was a workshop with a worn bench and a few rusty tools, nothing of value. The mowing machine, tedder, wagons and plow in the back of the barn were much the worse for wear. The teeth were out of the hand rake and the blade of the hoe was hanging from the handle. It didn't look as though Mr. Collins had farmed there for a long time. It was lucky the Woods had tools to work with.

Chip climbed the ladder to the mow and, trying to dodge the dirty, stringy cobwebs that hung from the rafters, he made his way to a door, lifted the latch, and went in. He found himself in a small room with two grimy, spider-webbed windows and small compartments built against one wall. A pigeon cote! He knew a boy who raised pigeons, and if they bought this place he could raise some, too, and make money. Oh, boy! He could hardly wait.

The only furniture was an old desk and a swivel chair. Chip dusted it with his handkerchief, sat down, tilted back and put his feet on the desk, feeling like the president of a giant corporation. This room would be his, his secret hide-away. He'd clean it, paint it, put pictures on

the wall, and use the desk for some of the things his
mother was always trying to get him to throw away.

He tugged at the bottom drawer and found it almost
too heavy to move. With growing excitement he pulled
harder and harder until, at last, it opened.

Remembering it afterwards, Chip wondered what he
had hoped to find inside. Treasure? Weapons? A map
with "X marks the spot?" It was none of those things,
only old seed catalogues. He felt a wave of disappointment and began to tug at the drawer above. It, too,
was heavy, filled to overflowing with Town Reports. He
heard the family coming and yanked at the next drawer.
Unless they bought the place he would never see this
room again, and he had to know what the old desk held.

With a last desperate pull he got the drawer open
and discovered bundles of letters there. He riffled the
edges of one pack, noticing the stamps and dates, 1946,
1945, 1944. Farther back were more packs, held with
rubber bands, brittle and broken. The one letter he pulled
out was a tax receipt for the year 1920; the green one-
cent stamps were pictures of the Mayflower. The year
1920! That was when his father was born! So long ago!
He heard the family coming nearer, and he closed the
drawer and made quick time down the ladder.

When they found him, Chip was examining the hay
rake. "The tools are no good, Dad," he said, trying to
keep his excitement from showing in his voice. "I think
our first investment ought to be a tractor."

"We'll see," his father answered. "Come on, now."
He turned to the agent. "Thank you for showing us

around. We'll talk it over, and as soon as we reach a decision we'll let you know."

"Take your time," Mr. Tower said with a smile. "Think it over as long as you wish. There is no hurry about making a decision."

No hurry? Chip wondered. That wasn't what Mr. Collins had said. He gave his father a questioning glance, but his father ignored it.

"We'll let you know very soon, Mr. Tower," he said, holding the front door open for his wife, while Chip and the girls scrambled into the back seat of the car.

"It's a very nice farm," Dolly screamed through the window. "If we buy it, I'm going to have a dog and a kitty like my mama had when she was a little girl."

For the first few miles everybody talked and nobody listened. Then Mr. and Mrs. Wood stopped talking to think about the decision they must make, the decision which would affect the lives of everyone in the car. Chip stopped talking to think about his secret room. He was lost in a dream of finding a rare old stamp worth ten thousand dollars when Dolly's whoop brought him back to reality.

"What's the matter with you?" he asked.

"We're going back!"

It was true. At least his father had pulled off the road and stopped the car.

"You can't keep on at the office, not with your eyes the way they are," Mrs. Wood was saying. "The children love the place, and it is a bargain at that price. I lived for years without a bathroom. I guess I can do it again."

"It'll be a hard life, Anna," her husband said. "I'm not asking you to do it. I'm not even sure I want to do it. Let's think it over for a while, unless..."

He left the sentence unfinished. On the back seat the three children sat like wooden Indians, waiting for the final word.

It came from Mother. "Go back, Charles," she said, "before those people Mr. Collins told you about get ahead of us."

CHAPTER FOUR

WEATHER VANE

To celebrate the important decision, they stopped at a little restaurant for hamburgers and ice cream. It was nearly dark when they reached home. Butch was waiting on the steps.

"Hi, Chip," he called, "I've got something to tell you."

"Yuh? I've got something to tell you, too. We just bought a farm."

"You did? Where?" He followed Chip into the garage.

"In Redfield."

"You mean you're going to live there?"

"Sure." Chip switched off the lights and locked the garage doors. "What's on your mind?"

"Joe Kelley was here looking for you. He's chosen us for Assistant Junior Counsellors at camp. For the whole ten weeks. Can you beat that?" The usually placid Butch was so overcome by the wonder of it that he could hardly

35

talk. "It won't cost us a cent, and you know how the
AJC's were last summer, having fun like everybody else.
Having more fun, really, because they could help the
chief and wear those letters on their jerseys."

He looked at Chip's long face. "What's the matter?
Don't you ... don't you want to go?" he asked unbeliev-
ingly.

"Of course I want to go." Camp Hokopoket! He had
had two happy weeks there, two weeks he would never
forget. He could almost smell the hot sun on pine needles,
hear the shouts of a hundred happy kids, and feel the
cool shock of a dive into the sparkling lake. Hikes. Camp-
fires. And Joe Kelley, their chief at camp; the same Joe
Kelley who was Mr. Kelley at Junior High, athletic super-
visor and the best science teacher in the whole United
States.

Chip swallowed the lump in his throat. "Maybe I
can go for a week," he said at last. "I can't go for all
summer."

"Why not? Just because your folks bought a farm,
you don't have to stay home all the time. This is like
earning money, because you are earning all your expenses,
five dollars a day. It's a job, Chip. You always wanted
to be an assistant. You said so." Butch kicked a round
hole in the gravel driveway. "You've got to go."

"When do I have to let him know?"

"I told him already. I said sure, we'd both go. We're
to help in the crafts room and teach new boys how to
make those little chairs like the one you made for Dolly.
You and me, Chip. Gee, we've always been together."

Butch's round blue eyes wandered over Chip's face trying to figure out what was wrong with him.

Chip was remembering his father's words: "You'll have to work." Work with spade and hoe, when he could be earning five dollars a day at Joe Kelley's camp. Weed, and transplant seedlings hour after hour, when he could be Assistant Junior Counsellor, with swimming and hiking a part of his duties. He sighed. Life was complicated. And how!

"What's the matter?" Butch asked. "Why don't you tell your father it won't cost anything?" His face brightened with a happy new idea. "Tell him it will save him money, because he won't have to feed you all summer."

"That might help, but when we have our farm, I've got to work. I'll call Joe Kelley and see if he'll take me for a week, or maybe the last two weeks of August."

"He will. It's like a scholarship or something that pays the expenses of the AJC's. You can go part time. Come over to my house and call him up now."

Chip's spirits rose as they crossed the street. It would work out all right to go the last two weeks of August. There would be plenty of time to tell his father later. By the time Chip had talked to Joe Kelley, he could already see that AJC on his blue jersey.

The next morning when he awoke, he had one minute of panic. He should have asked his father, for going off to camp was just the sort of thing his father had meant he couldn't do, if they bought the farm. He wriggled down in the bed, flopped over on his face, and moved his thoughts from troubles to the farm. The Charles

Augustus Woods owned—or at least had made a down payment on—a farm, a hill, a brook, a barn with a secret room and a drawer full of old, old stamps. Why worry about August?

He jumped out of bed and shivered. It was snowing hard.

"Crazy weather," he growled, slamming the window down and grabbing his clothes to dress in the bathroom where it was warm.

When he came out, Dolly, in her long red robe and bunny slippers, her curly black hair standing on end, was shouting through the bedroom door to her father.

"No," he answered, "we are not going to the farm today. You can go to Sunday School, but there's no point in driving to Redfield in the snow."

Chip spent the morning with his stamps. He had a good collection. Some were those his father had saved when he was a boy or had salvaged from office letters from all parts of the world. Chip had bought others at the Five and Ten, and had sent away for special offers. It had been months since he had thought about them but as he looked them over and then checked his catalogue for the values of old stamps the time passed quickly.

Tired of sitting still so long, he went to the window and stretched. The snow had stopped. He decided to shovel it off the sidewalk and drive. He ran downstairs to the living room, where his father was at work, his desk and the card table covered with papers.

"Dad, why didn't you tell me you were doing reports? I wanted to read off figures while you check."

"I didn't want to disturb you. You were doing your homework, weren't you?" He took off his glasses and rubbed his eyes. "You mustn't get discouraged about your English. It's the one subject you must master, no matter where you go to school. If I can help you, let me know."

"I haven't done it yet."

Mr. Wood looked at his son thoughtfully. "Where are you going?"

"I thought I'd shovel snow a while." Chip looked through the window at Carol and Dolly, who were making a snowman, and at Butch, who had come over to help. This would be a good time to talk with his father about going to camp, but Chip's feet carried him right along and out the door.

It was Thursday before the Woods got to Redfield again. That night they carried their supper and ate it in the living room, standing around a cheery fireplace. Then Mr. Wood left to find a man to do the plowing, Mrs. Wood began to take measurements to see where her furniture would go, and Chip and the girls ran outdoors towards the barn.

As he looked up, Chip felt a prickly chill zip down his spine. He left his sisters and tramped around the barn through the wet snow and then backed off and looked up again.

The ship, the golden ball, the four gold letters N, S, E,W—everything was gone!

"Did somebody steal it?" Dolly asked.

"Yes. It hasn't blown off. And there aren't any footprints in the snow, so it must have been stolen last Saturday night."

"Daddy's back. I'm going to tell him," Dolly cried. They followed her to the house where they found Mr. Tower in the kitchen talking with their father.

"What's the matter?" their father asked when he saw their excited faces. They all talked at once, but the meaning was clear. Somebody had stolen their weathervane.

"No," Mr. Tower said, stroking his left hand as though it were a kitten. "I had a man take it down. Mr. Collins gave it to me when he left, and I have been negligent about having it moved. It is now on my garage."

Chip's face fell. "May I take measurements and see if I can make one? The barn looks kind of bare now. She was such a beautiful ship. Dad, we saw one in that antique shop on the Cape, don't you remember? And the man said it was a model of the *Flying Cloud,* and it was so valuable it wasn't even for sale. Does this ship have a name, Mr. Tower?"

"Not that I know of." He looked at Chip with a one-sided smile. "Are you especially interested in ships?"

"Yes. I'm interested in just about everything."

"You said it," his father agreed with a proud glance at his son. "If Mr. Tower is willing, we'll take the lines off her, and I'll help you make another for our barn. It will be good work for us during the long winter evenings."

"How old are you?" Mr. Tower asked.

"Nearly fourteen."

"I have a son, sixteen."

"Have you any little girls?" Dolly asked.

"I have one daughter, twelve."

"I'm nearly twelve," Carol volunteered.

"And I'm five." Dolly whirled around on her tiptoes until she was dizzy.

"Does your boy go to high school?" Chip asked, surprised to find that Mr. Tower had children. He didn't look like any of the fathers Chip knew.

"No. Judson attends Barton Academy. Sharon's at Miss Houghton's school."

"Why? Aren't the Redfield schools any good?" Chip asked.

"I presume they are. But Mrs. Tower and I travel a great deal. That is one reason we prefer to have our children attend private schools."

There was something about Mr. Tower Chip did not like. Not just the way he moved his hands when he talked, or smiled with his mouth but not with his eyes, but something deeper. Sensitively aware of people's feelings under what seemed like friendly faces, Chip knew that Mr. Tower had never wanted them to buy the farm. That is why he had said there was no hurry about making a decision, no hurry at all. He did not want them to live so near to his own house.

And the weathervane. Of course he had a right to it if Mr. Collins had given it to him, but Chip wished he had taken it down before their first visit. It belonged on the lofty cupola, not on the garage of a modern ranch house.

Well, he decided, he'd make a new weathervane. Boy! Would he be busy from here on!

Busy was too small a word to describe the days that followed.

From early morning until late at night he was rushing every minute.

There were a hundred things to be done at home, another hundred at the farm, and a hundred interruptions. One day it was company. First to arrive were Miss Hattie and Miss Mattie Morgan, retired school teachers, who lived in the only other house on Stonybrook Lane. They had brought a box of strawberries for the Woods' supper; they invited them to attend services at the Redfield Church; they asked Chip to help them with their chores.

They had hardly gone when a car drove in bringing the Haydens, a young colored man and his wife and their two little children. They were pleasant, too, and they asked Carol to help them with the babies. Both she and Chip were planning how to spend all the money they would earn when their father reminded them that for some time they would be working for him, Chip in the fields and Carol tending a stand under the elm tree.

She and Chip didn't argue, but they were sure there would be time for both.

There was a pattern to the days, but many of them had high spots. There was the day the papers were signed;

the day they turned their car in for a station wagon so that they could move the garden stuff and much of the furniture themselves; the day the King Street house was sold and Chip's mother cried, and Chip wanted to; and the Friday when they camped out at the farm all night, getting up at five the next morning to begin a big day's work.

That was the weekend Chip decided he had misjudged Mr. Tower, for he offered the Woods a camp cot and a table to make their staying overnight more comfortable. On Saturday afternoon, glad to stretch his legs after helping his father lay the kitchen linoleum, Chip walked over to the Towers' house to see when they could call for the things. There was no one on the road. It was a glorious feeling, having the whole world to himself.

Birds were singing everywhere, so Chip sang, too, louder and louder, until he came within sight of the long, low ranch house. He walked slowly up the drive, studying the ship on the garage. It was larger than he had thought, at least thirty inches long. The sail was metal, the ropes, wire. It was so delicately balanced on its golden ball that it veered with every whiff of wind.

He heard a vacuum cleaner humming inside the house, so he knocked loudly on the door. A pretty, plump little woman opened it. Chip was pleasantly surprised as she smiled at him.

"Good afternoon," he said, "your husband said he had some things for us. We'll come with our station wagon any time you say." She looked as though she didn't understand, so Chip added, "I'm Chip Wood, from the Collins' place."

"Sure," she said. "Come in. I'm not Mrs. Tower. I'm Inga Paulson. I work here. I'm glad a family with children is moving into that house. Have a cookie."

"Thank you," Chip said, as the brittle ginger cookie broke in his fingers. "Mm! Pepperkoker!"

"You know pepperkoker?" she exclaimed, opening her blue eyes wide in surprise.

"Yes. Butch Swanson's mother makes them. He's my pal in Courtney. He's Swedish. Are you?"

She was Swedish. She was interested in hearing all about Chip's family, and he was glad to tell her, eating cookies all the while.

They were having a fine chat when a strident voice demanded, "What is going on out here?" Chip didn't need to be told that this was Mrs. Tower. She was a large woman with prominent blue eyes and reddish yellow hair, and she wore a bright flowered housecoat that swept the floor and added to her majesty.

"I'm Chip Wood," he said, swallowing the last cookie fast. "Is Mr. Tower ready for us to come for the table and cot he said we could have?"

"Oh." She looked Chip over thoroughly from his short black hair and much-mended sweater to the faded dungarees and worn sneakers. Then she called, "Judson, that Negro boy is here. What shall I tell him?"

"Everything's ready. They're in the garage. Tell him to come any time," a voice from another room replied.

"Thank you," Chip said. He turned to Mrs. Paulson and said it again, and that time he smiled.

All the way home he tried to pin down just what it was about the Towers that he didn't like. Would the son, Judson, be friendly, he wondered. He wondered all the way home.

CHAPTER FIVE

SHARON

By the end of May the Woods were half moved. Every weekend, and nearly every night after their father came home from work, they loaded the station wagon and drove the fourteen miles to the farm. They could cook, eat, work and sleep in either place. It was a gypsy life. Chip and the girls loved it.

The days continued to be full from dawn to evening. There was papering and painting to be done, floors to be scrubbed and painted and waxed, and one room after another made ready for the furniture. Dead grass and rubble must be raked and burned, a vegetable garden started, the pansy plants and violets and perennials in the Courtney lot had to be sold or moved. Chip spent hours pricking out zinnia and marigold seedlings and getting them into seed flats, while his father and the man he hired got the big fields ready for dahlias, gladioli and

sweet peas, which they had decided to specialize in this
first year.

Chip was on his knees transplanting lettuce one night,
when Mrs. Paulson called to him. "I know how hard it
is to try to live in two places at once," she said, and
she showed him a coffee cake and a pot of beans she
had baked for his mother.

"Won't you come in?" he asked, wiping his hands on
his dungarees and taking the heavy beanpot as he led
the way to the house. He opened the door and stepped
back for her to enter, then introduced his mother and
sisters.

"Thank you so much. Can't you sit down while I
make coffee?" Mrs. Wood asked, tears in her eyes at this
proof of friendliness. "Please excuse the looks of this
kitchen, but I'm so glad to have someone to talk to,
that's all that matters. You children run out and play."

"I want to ask her something first," Chip insisted.
"What's the Tower boy like? Is he friendly, or is he . . .?"

While Chip searched for the right word, Inga Paulson
sucked in her cheeks and looked at the ceiling. "I doubt
if you'll see much of Jud," she said. "He's a lot older
than you. You know, with all their money, I wouldn't
change places with any of those Towers."

"Why not?"

"They don't have fun. They don't laugh, or sing, or
tell funny stories. They've got some money, and that's
all they've got." She shrugged her shoulders and lifted
her hands in a gesture that meant it was an empty life.
"Ten years I've been with them, and believe me, I know.

Jud Tower wants his children to have the best of everything, but he don't understand them. They don't get
along together." She shook her head and nibbled the crisp
cookie Mrs. Wood offered her.

The children got one, too, and Mrs. Wood nodded
toward the door. But there was no getting rid of them,
or stopping Inga's flow of gossip.

"You know, that Sharon," she went on, "she gets mad,
and then gets over it. But young Jud shuts up like a clam,
and nobody can get a word out of him. He's an awful
disappointment to his father. Sharon's sassy, but she
means all right. I'm fond of her."

"When will she come home?" Carol asked.

"Next week. You know, you'd be good for Sharon.
I hope you two will be friends."

"I hope so, too. Is she pretty?"

Chip mimicked her. "Is she pretty? What difference
does that make? You like Joanie, and she looks like a
Disney duck."

"Why, Chip Wood, she does not."

"She does too. What about the boy? Is he pretty?"
he teased.

"I hope he's a pretty boy," Dolly echoed.

"That's enough," their mother said. "Out you go. All
of you."

Apparently he couldn't count on the Tower boy for
a pal, but Chip had too much on his mind to think any
more about it. He had never felt as well as he did that
spring. Boundless energy flowed through him. The more

he did, the more he wanted to do. The new house in the country was fast becoming a home.

The burst of enthusiasm was evident in school, too. His marks were improving, even in English. He felt wide awake, hitting on all eight cylinders. Baseball was out, of course, and for several weeks he kept away from Freddy Greer.

The days flew by too fast for counting. The chance to get up to his room in the barn, to look at his stamps, had to be pushed further and further ahead. He did manage to put a padlock on the door without anyone's discovering it, but the few times he had stolen away someone was always looking for him, usually Dolly.

He had opened one packet of letters and found the receipted bills for grain and vegetable seed were dated 1912, 1913, and the stamps were issues of Balboa, Marquette, and the Panama canal; pretty stamps, but with no special value. Well, he hadn't half looked yet. It was a temptation to take the letters to his bedroom, but they were hard to conceal, and part of the pleasure was keeping it secret.

Another discovery was the long top drawer above the other three. It was locked, and all Chip's efforts to open it were unsuccessful. After he broke his good scout knife trying to pry it open, he gave up, until he could get the proper tools. There would be plenty of chances later.

A few days after that, they were on the porch eating a sandwich supper, when a long red car drove in, spitting gravel as it made a quick stop. A boy was driving. The

tall thin girl beside him slid out quickly and came toward
the steps. She wore tight blue ranch pants and a long-
sleeved black sweater which emphasized her tallness and
thinness. Her light hair was pulled back from her face
and tied in a pony tail; her eyes were blue and her
mouth was painted fire-truck red.

"Hello," she said, seating herself on the lower step
where she could look up at them. "I'm Sharon Tower.
The stationary object in the car is my darling brother
Jud, otherwise known as Junior."

They all looked at Jud, who scowled darkly, and lit
a cigarette without acknowledging the introduction. "J.P.
—that's my father, of course—told me about you, so
I came to look you over."

The Woods stopped eating their sandwiches and
stared.

"J.P.'s got himself a new pair of ulcers, worrying over
you," she continued.

"Why should he worry over us?" Mr. Wood asked.
"I can assure you we're harmless."

Sharon met his eyes for a minute, then shrugged.
"Oh, he worries about everything." She gave him a quick
smile. "You know, I thought you'd be different, but
you talk like everybody else."

"Why shouldn't we?" Chip burst out. "Did you think
all colored people talk like Amos and Andy? We're no
different from anybody else."

"The way you're talking will never convince her of
that," his father said sternly. "What Chip means is that
all of us, and our parents and grandparents, have lived

in Courtney all our lives. So, naturally, we talk like other people who live around here."

"Of course. You would." Sharon smiled at Dolly and touched her hand. Dolly, always friendly, began to play with the bangles on Sharon's bracelet.

"Do you like it?" Sharon asked. "Do you want it?" She slipped it off and put it on Dolly's wrist.

"Look, Mama," Dolly cried, waving her arm in the air.

"Give it back to her," Mrs. Wood said.

"No, she can keep it. It's not valuable, and I've got lots more. I want her to have it because she's so cute." She pulled Dolly onto her lap, and her smile swept over them all. "I want to be friends with you. I love flowers, and I want to help you with your garden. I love working in the dirt."

"Give the bracelet back to the girl, Dolly," Mrs. Wood repeated sternly, and reluctantly Dolly did.

Sharon began to argue, but her words were drowned by a blast on the horn. "Yes, Juney, I'm coming. Juney's his baby name, and he adores it, don't you, darling?" she asked, as she walked to the car.

"Get in or walk home," he growled.

"Somebody in the family has to welcome the new people." She turned and waved. "'Bye. I'll be over again tomorrow." Jud slammed the car into high gear and they roared away.

"The less we see of that girl the better I'll like it," Mrs. Wood declared.

"Oh, she's got style, mother," Carol answered. "She

looks like the girls in *Seventeen,* her hair, her clothes and everything."

"Carol," her mother scolded, "you keep away from her. You hear me? I won't have a rude, spoiled brat putting foolish ideas into your head. Only twelve years old and her mouth all painted and . . ."

"She isn't putting ideas into my head," Carol interrupted. "Oh, I wish I were thin so I could wear ranch pants."

"She was going to give me that pretty bracelet. I like her," Dolly stated.

"Raspberries," Chip growled, getting up to take his cup to the kitchen. "She pretended to like us, but she was making fun of us underneath. She's nuts, absolutely nuts, if you ask me."

"No, I don't agree," his father said. "I think she was curious, but I think she meant to be friendly. Now we all have different opinions. I wonder who will turn out to be right."

"You'll see who is right," his wife answered. "You'll see."

CHAPTER SIX

JUNE

June was divided into two parts. During the first half, the days were so full and flew by so fast that Chip could hardly believe the calendar. He got up early; dug into his books every study period, cramming for exams; made every minute in school count; then came home to another set of duties; and then went on to still different ones at the farm.

There everything needed doing at once. Weeds sprang up in the garden and grew like mad. Dahlia clumps which were still unplanted shot out long pale sprouts, begging to be divided into separate toes and given their chance in the good earth.

Every bug, worm and caterpillar in the neighborhood heard the good news that something was doing at the old Collins place, and they came in droves. Spraying had to be done at once. It was hard, heavy work when done by hand, tank on shoulder, or lugging a bucket. Often Chip was so weary he fell asleep on the ride back to Courtney.

But it wasn't all work. The weekend he celebrated his fourteenth birthday he invited Butch and six other boys to the farm for overnight. They had a grand time. They blazed a trail to an old wood lot. They roamed the woods and hiked to the top of Redfield's highest hill. At night they slept out under the stars.

Chip always remembered that night. For a long time he lay awake, looking up into the sky and wondering what the year would bring. It would be different from all his other years. He had reached a parting of the ways. He thought of his father's words, and wished that he could see a year, two years ahead.

These boys had been his friends, his good friends, especially Butch. What would it be like at the new school? Would the Redfield boys accept him? Or would he be left out of things? What about Joe Kelley's camp? What about college? So many questions without answers! Well, this year would answer some of them. He moved his sleeping bag to a more nearly level place, and stared at the stars another hour before he fell asleep.

The biggest event of all was the farewell party the office gave for Mr. Wood. The family was invited. They glowed with pride as people said nice things about Mr. Wood and presented him with a beautiful chair and footstool. When he made his thank-you speech, he asked all of them to visit Redfield and see the new flower fields.

Many of them came. So did friends from King Street,

and aunts and uncles and grandparents and all kinds of relatives. So, added to the work, were the visitors. And in the middle of everything, was Sharon Tower. Chip's mother did not like it; Sharon's parents didn't either, but it made no difference to her. She was determined to be friendly; she was determined to help.

Nearly every afternoon when they arrived at Redfield, she was there waiting, dressed in dungarees and one of Jud's old shirts. Carol, who had never done it before, worked along with her, hoeing, or weeding, or picking Hessian bugs off the roses and peonies if that was what needed to be done.

One night, as they were transplanting petunias to a new plot under the bay window, Chip overheard Sharon talking about the camp where she went each summer. Because he was interested in camping, he hung around to listen.

"They have good horses," Sharon was saying, "and that is absolutely the only good thing. The woman who runs it is a bird, and I mean bird. She looks like a heron with a long skinny neck and a nose like a beak. We have to work with clay. Imagine that, like babies. Anyway, I modeled her, even the heron legs. It was good, too."

"You didn't!" Carol gasped, admiringly.

"Oh yes I did. I got sent home, but I plan to get sent home every summer. Then I go to Maine. We have a nice little place there. J.P. and the Queen—I call my mother that to flatter her—they go every August. It's too boring to stay a month, but I like to look in on them."

While she talked, she moved each plant carefully, untangling the threadlike roots and setting it exactly eight inches from the others. Carol, awkward and slow, stopped her work to watch, adoration in her eyes.

"Oh, Sharon, look at all you've done, and they're so even," she said with a sigh. "You're good at everything."

"I'm good at doing things I like, and I like to work outdoors with flowers. It isn't very often I have the chance. Somebody's always trying to boss me. My father wouldn't let me touch a plant in our garden. Do you know what I'd really like to do?" She waved her hands, still full of wet earth, towards the flower fields. "I'd like to stay home this summer and work here every day. I mean it, Carol. Work, really work. I suppose J.P. would be horrified if I asked him. Your mother wouldn't like it either, or your brother, the sour old pie-eye."

Chip, still within hearing distance, thought that over for a while. He'd like to tell her what he thought about her cheap talk. Always raving about how smart she was. Still, she had a real knack for gardening. She was a big help, so he kept quiet. That first half of June was so full of so many things that anything Sharon said got jammed down into the bottom of his mind with the other disagreeable things he would like to forget, such as telling his father about camp, and Stringer's final English test.

Actually, he had high hopes of passing that test. Then Butch, of all people, got him so upset he could hardly remember his own name.

For weeks Chip had been going out of his way to avoid Freddy Greer. So, when he saw him with Butch,

Chip went to the lunch room alone. He had nearly finished eating when his pal came in.

"What's Freddy want?" he asked.

"Nothing." Butch answered unhappily.

"Look, you aren't fooling me. What's up?" Chip insisted.

"He was talking about you and your farm."

"What about it? Butch, you've got to tell me."

"I don't think I ought to. He's an awful liar, and he probably made it up." Butch chewed his milk straw until it hung, flat and wilted, over the edge of the bottle.

"I know he's a liar, but what's that got to do with our farm?"

"You know the day we played Redfield High? Freddy talked to a boy."

"So what?" Chip urged him on.

"He says they stuck your father on the price. He says they've been trying to sell that place for years, even before the old man moved out, and anybody could have bought it for five thousand dollars, but when . . . when Mr. Collins saw your father he raised it. Look out. Here comes Freddy."

"Talking about me?" Freddy sneered. "Do you have to tell everything you know?"

"He told me," Chip retorted, "just like you meant for him to. But it isn't true. I don't believe a word of it."

Freddy laughed and poked him in the ribs with a long finger.

"Ask anybody in Redfield," he said, "anybody at all."

Chip went to his English test the next period with
Freddy's laugh ringing in his ears. How he hated that
guy! He hoped that when he moved to Redfield he'd
never see him or hear of him again. Mixed with the
hatred was a sick feeling. His father had trusted Mr.
Collins. He had believed Mr. Collins wanted him to buy
the place. Could it be the old man was two-faced, pretending to be friendly when he wasn't? There must have
been some truth in what Freddy said—ask anybody in
Redfield, anybody at all.

Chip looked at the mimeographed sheet that Mr.
Stringer laid on his desk and tried to concentrate. It
was no use. He couldn't think. It was all he could do to
sit still and watch the rest of the class scribbling away
as the minutes ticked by. He leaned his chin on his fist
and scowled at Mr. Stringer, who pointed at the clock
as a warning.

He hated Stringer. He hated Freddy, and Mr. Collins
and the Towers and everybody in Redfield. What was
the use of trying so hard? What was the use?

The period was half over before he wrote a word on
his paper. The bell rang before he finished the questions
he did know. A wild impulse came over him to tear up
his paper and throw it at the teacher, but he shoved it
across Stringer's desk and went out into the hall.

In spite of it, he hoped his daily work would pull
him through. It didn't. Two days before school closed
he got his report card with its red D. And that marked
the beginning of the second half of June. Mr. Wood
got through at the office. The electric stove, refrigerator,

and other heavy things, came by truck from the King
Street house, and the Woods settled down in Redfield
to stay.

It took a few days to get used to it, and then Chip
slumped. Butch went to camp; so did Sharon. Carol took
a trip to the White Mountains with Joanie's family. But
Chip stayed on the farm with the bugs, the weeds and
the work. He was tired from the top of his head to the
soles of his feet; tired, let-down and unhappy.

One afternoon as he was picking peas to take to Inga
Paulson, in return for her many kindnesses, Mr. and Mrs.
Tower drove into the yard.

"Is your mother at home?" Mrs. Tower asked, giving
Chip a snobbish look.

He took them to the house and called his mother.
He hung around to find out why they had come, but it
was apparently a courtesy call, mixed with curiosity. Mrs.
Tower looked around the pleasant living room, and un-
bent enough to admire the hooked rugs Chip's mother
had made.

Mrs. Wood smiled politely and thanked Mrs. Tower
for her praise, but Chip noticed she did not ask them to
have coffee, and Dolly, feeling the restraint, sat quietly
in the little chair Chip had made for her. When they
were ready to go, Mrs. Tower looked into the kitchen.
She saw the pump at the sink.

"I thought you had water put in," she exclaimed.
"How do you manage without plumbing? I'm afraid I'm
spoiled. We have a bath and shower with every bedroom.
It was one of the things I insisted on when our house

was built. But I suppose you're like the Collinses. They preferred their old-fashioned ways."

Chip's mother put on a frozen smile as she explained they were not used to old-fashioned ways, and that they would have water installed just as soon as they could pay for it.

Mr. Tower turned to Chip. "How would you like to earn a couple of dollars a week cutting our grass?" he asked. "A big boy like you should do something to help out."

"I do help. I'm pretty busy, but maybe I can do it."

It was the worst deal he ever made, for the couple of dollars meant just that, two. The lawn was large, and there were edges to be trimmed. And Jud, the lazy fish-face, sat in the lawn chair smoking while Chip worked.

During those last weeks of June and early July it seemed as though nothing was right. For one thing, he was lonesome. When he went to the store or the post office, people looked at him and half smiled, but nobody spoke, and he didn't want to speak first. Occasionally he stole away to his room in the barn, but it was stiflingly hot up there with the windows closed, and he couldn't open them without being discovered. He looked forward to a cool, rainy day, and when one came, he took his stamp catalogues to the barn and disappeared. He hadn't been in his room ten minutes when he heard Dolly.

"Chip, where did you go?" she called.

At first he didn't answer, but, as she kept calling,

he opened the door. She was halfway up the ladder.

"What's up there?" she asked.

"Cobwebs and dirt," he told her, stepping out and locking the door quickly. "Now look, it's easy climbing up the ladder, but going down is dangerous, and there are holes in the floor boards up here." She backed down as he descended. He took her by the shoulder. "Promise me you won't go up there."

She wriggled free. "You went up."

"But you're not going. Understand?"

"I won't go unless you're there. Then you can help me down." She looked at him, then at the ladder. "Anyway, Mama wants you to help Daddy move a bed."

"You're a pest. That's what you are."

"So are you," she answered.

Chip crowded his anger down as he followed her back to the house. On the whole farm there was not one place he could call his own. His mother cleaned every inch of his bedroom, and it would not be long before Dolly found his hide-away. He needed a secret place, because as much as he liked his family, there were times when he wanted to be by himself.

His promise to Joe Kelley lurked in the back of his mind. That was something he ought to talk over with his father. But there was always work enough for six men, and the right time to talk didn't come.

July's hot days followed one another monotonously. Many gardens suffered, but the Towers kept sprinklers going, and Chip knew their grass needed cutting, so he went over. As he rolled out the lawn mower, Jud strolled up to him. "I met a fellow last night who knows you," he said. "His name's Freddy Greer."

Freddy Greer again! It was funny how this one guy he especially detested kept coming back into his life. "Yuh? I've known him a long time."

"I met him at a party," Jud went on. "A fellow I know introduced me because next year Freddy's going to Barton."

"Barton Academy?"

"Yuh, the brain factory where they'll keep any dope until he's ready for college—if the old man's money holds out. That's why I'm there."

"But Freddy told everybody he was going to Harvard next year."

"He couldn't get into Harvard."

Chip crossed the lawn and back. Jud was waiting for him. He knocked the ashes from his pipe. "I thought you'd want to know he remembered you," he said with a short laugh, and went into the house.

Chip wondered what else Freddy had said. Jud must know, everybody in Redfield must know about Mr. Collins' raising the price of the farm, Chip thought bitterly.

Money. If your dad had money you could succeed whether you worked or not. But if you were colored and didn't have money . . . He stopped to mop the sweat from his face. He and his father talked man to man about expenses, and Chip knew how near the zero point their present family income stood. He was in a jam all right. Not a chance of college, or camp, or anything.

When he got home that night, with two dollars in his pocket for over three hours hard work, he stalked through the living room without speaking. In his own room he pulled a sheet of paper and envelope from a box.

"Dear Joe Kelley," he wrote, "I cannot be Assistant Junior Counsellor in August because I have to work all the time for my father."

"Where are you going, dear? It's late," his mother said as he went out to mail it. The slamming door was her only answer.

CHAPTER SEVEN

STAMPS

It took a new friendship to lift Chip from his gloomy mood. Sometimes after supper he rode his bike down the hill to Legion Park, where the town boys played ball. He spoke to no one; no one spoke to him. But on the third night, one of the players, a fellow who reminded him a little of Butch, got to talking with him. It didn't take them long to get acquainted.

"Want to play?" the boy asked. "We can use all the players we can get."

"Sure, I'll play," Chip said, as a little peanut hit a home run and ran the bases like a greyhound, while the crowd cheered and half the team left the field to hunt for the ball. This was what he had missed: the shouting and the razzing, the companionship of boys.

"Well, come on. What are you waiting for? My name's Pat Moore. What's yours?"

"Chip Wood."

He went in and played a good game and felt better. The fellows asked him to come again, and Chip did, whenever he could get away. Pat Moore became a real friend. He was sixteen, older than he looked, and he had an old jalopy and a boat with an outboard motor.

One afternoon he asked Chip to go fishing. The pond was a few miles north of Redfield, and for Chip it was a treat to be going somewhere. He caught two bass and a brown trout that first day. After that Pat asked him often, and Chip always begged off from his work to go, explaining that the fish helped out on the food budget. He would have gone every day in the week if he could have. The family was glad he didn't.

"Fish again?" Carol complained one night at supper. "I'm getting awfully sick of fish."

"I'm sick of fish, too. I don't like fish at all," Dolly echoed.

"Listen, you two. I catch 'em and I clean 'em, and the least you can do is eat 'em," Chip exploded.

"Stop wrangling," his mother interrupted. "What this family needs is a change, a holiday. We've all been working too hard and not getting out enough."

"So what?" Chip asked.

"Thursday is Grandma's birthday. We'll leave as soon as you get the flowers picked for the florist, and spend the day in Courtney with her."

"Not me," Chip said promptly. "I'm not going."

"Oh, Chip." His mother looked at him with worry in her eyes. "Why do you talk like that? I can't understand you sometimes."

"Somebody should stay here," he declared, "and it's
going to be me."

"What would you do all day alone? You need a day
off as much as any of us."

"I'll find plenty to do."

"Okay. You stay," his father agreed. "We might have
some customers. But take it easy. You need a rest, like
your mother says."

"His grandmother won't like it. She'll want to see
Chip," Mrs. Wood began.

"Anna," her husband broke in, "the boy's tired. He
needs a day by himself. When all the family get to talking,
it's not especially restful. Let him stay home and be
quiet."

Chip began to count the days to Thursday, happier
than he had been all summer.

The minute the family car was out of sight, he ran
to the barn with hammer and chisel, opened the
windows wide, and went to work on the top desk drawer.
He banged with all his might, enjoying the noise, feeling
more cheerful with every blow. Finally the old wood
broke from the lock, and he pulled the drawer free.

Inside was a bundle of letters, a letter-paper box, and
an old, bulging brown notebook, its cover bearing the
words, "Pierce's Memorandum and Account Book, de-
signed for Farmers, Mechanics and *All People*," and at
the top, in faded letters, *SETH COLLINS' STAMPS*.

As he turned the yellowed pages, Chip's excitement
rose to fever pitch. Here was real treasure—rows of blue
Franklins, the cancellations marked by hand with pen

and ink, a page of Washingtons, dark green, light blue, dark blue, red, brown.

What years, what values? he wondered. At the top of each page was a tiny monthly calendar for 1886 and 1887, so they were probably eighteen-eighty's, the Garfields, Lincolns, Taylors, Grants. He reached for the box, opened it, and almost stopped breathing. The top envelope had a red three-cent Washington, cut diagonally, and bearing the cancellation "Redfield," the "Redf-" on the envelope, the other letters on the stamp. A bisect! That was worth big money, Chip knew. It was for only a short time that it was legal to cut stamps in that way. Apparently Mr. Collins knew he had some prizes, for with it was another cover with a diagonal half, a twelve-cent black Washington, worth possibly five hundred dollars. And there were more, many more.

Chip took a deep breath and looked out the window, where goldfinches in undulating flight twittered from apple tree to sky. That collection was worth at least a thousand dollars, probably much more. Enough for college, or a tractor, or an electric pump and water system, a shower and a nice tiled bath like the one they'd had in Courtney. Or enough for a greenhouse and a man to help with the work, so Chip could go to camp after all. He let his thoughts roam, dipping and rising as the goldfinches did, and dipping again because there was a question he must answer: were they really his to keep?

He felt a weight like a lead sinker where his stomach was supposed to be; his conscience probably, fighting it out with his common sense, which said they had bought

the place and everything on it belonged to them. Yes,
and they'd paid plenty, too. They certainly owed Mr.
Collins nothing.

He looked again at the funny little notebook, its left-
hand pages bearing advertisements of remedies "for every
sickness known to man or beast." He looked at the
stamps, stuck in with hand-made tabs. No gummed
hinges in those days, or stamp albums, or if there were,
young Seth Collins had not been able to afford them.

Before going to the house for his catalogue Chip
untied one bundle of letters. On top was a postcard from
Cpl. Seth Collins, Jr., Co. L., 302nd Infantry, American
Expeditionary Force, France. Chip saw the red triangle
of the YMCA, and read the message that told of the
boy's safe arrival. The year was 1917! Whew! Over forty
years ago! He looked at the brown envelopes over-
printed in green, marked *ACTIVE SERVICE*. They were
so worn and frayed at the edges that they were ready
to fall apart.

Chip sat staring at them. What had happened? Had
the son been killed, or was he the one Mr. Collins lived
with now? And why had the old man kept the letters
locked up in this desk in the barn, and left them there?
Had he come here to read them, so his wife wouldn't
know? And then forgotten them?

I suppose I should return them, Chip thought. But
how could he return the letters without returning the
stamps?

Restlessness drove him to action. He was in no mood
to sit down and study a stamp catalogue. Instead, he

went to the store and bought a padlock for the desk, returned and mended the drawer by nailing a cleat across the front. Then he brushed down the windows and walls and swept the floor, tacked up a magazine cover he had saved because the boy on it looked like Butch, and other pictures of planes and baseball players, and a large picture map of New England.

He found an empty crate, and made a shelf for it, and filled it with old copies of magazines that he had stowed away in his bedroom closet. Later he would put up a lot of shelves, build himself a bunk bed and a table.

The hours flew by, but he kept track of the time. When the family got home, they found him cutting the grass.

"We had fun, Chip," Dolly cried, running up with a piece of birthday cake.

"What did you do all day?" his mother asked.

"Nothing much." He grinned and walked away.

After that, the room was always at the top of his thoughts. His conscience soon accepted the idea that the stamps were his, and he longed for an opportunity to verify watermarks, imperforations and variations in shading between originals and reprints. The old blue Franklins were issue of 1870, he discovered, and listed at only thirty cents each, which was disappointing, but a buff five-cent Jefferson was worth thirty dollars, and the red bisect, if it was 1857 as he suspected, was probably worth more than any of the others. So he studied his catalogue, and dreamed his dreams.

CHAPTER EIGHT

SECRETS

For a week he found no chance to visit his hide-away without danger of being discovered. Joanie had come to visit Carol. The two were so busy talking secrets while they tended the roadside stand under the elm tree, that Dolly was lonesome. So she tagged after Chip most of the time.

One day his father went to Courtney, and Chip saw the girls with his mother busily sewing, Dolly for her doll, the other two on dresses for school. He took a chance; with his catalogue under his arm, he went to the barn to check stamps against price lists.

He was deeply absorbed in the intricate differences in the 1882 issues, when a board creaked and he looked up. Dolly stood in the doorway, a naked doll dangling from her hand.

"You little snooper," he cried angrily, "what do you think you're doing up here?"

"What do you think you're doing?" she repeated saucily.

"It's none of your business. Didn't I tell you to keep off that ladder?"

"But I didn't fall," she interrupted, climbing into his lap. "Oh, stamps," she said. She'd seen his stamps before, so she wriggled down and walked around the room to look at the pictures he had tacked on the wall.

"This is a nice room and I like it," she declared. "But it's too hot. Why don't you open the windows?"

"Because I don't want anybody to know about it. But they'll all know now. You could never keep a secret."

"Yes I can." In his lap again, she grabbed him around the neck and hissed in his ear, "I won't tell anybody, not even Mama. Then can I come with you when you come up here?"

"No, you can't." He pulled her off and set her on her feet. "You know what you are? A pest. A prize pest."

He put the stamps away, locked up, and helped Dolly down the ladder. He stood a minute looking at it, and sighed. There was only one safe thing to do. She'd been up once; she'd certainly do it again. He tipped the rickety old ladder sideways and laid it on the floor.

"Why did you do that?" she asked.

"Because you are *not* going up there. Understand?"

"Oh yes I am, when you do, because then the ladder will be up again!" Her eyes were dancing as she turned and raced towards the house shouting, "Chip and I have a secret, but I'm not going to tell."

She didn't. Not that day.

The following night, at supper, Carol was quietly stating all the reasons why Chip should take them to a lawn party at the Grange Hall. Dolly was teasing, and Joanie was interrupting with giggles and suggestions, while Chip ate his ham cakes and cole slaw quickly and silently.

"Chip, I think you ought to go," his mother chimed in. "I don't want the girls to go alone, but all of you together could have a good time."

"Do I have to?" Chip groaned.

Dolly piped up, "I know why he doesn't want to go." She slid out of her chair, rushed to him, and whispered loudly in his ear.

"Secrets?" his father asked, smiling.

"Dolly, sit down," Chip ordered.

"But I want to ask you something," she insisted, grabbing him around the neck.

While the others raved about the lawn party, Chip laid down his knife and fork and pulled Dolly's arms away.

"Finish your supper, Dolly," Mr. Wood demanded. "And you girls keep quiet a minute. I want to ask Chip something. Why did you take the ladder down from the mow?"

"Because Dolly's always climbing up there, and if she falls off she'll break her neck. I've told her twice not to do it."

Dolly cried, "You told part of our secret. Now can I tell part?"

Chip glared at her. "Go ahead. Tell it all. Tell everything you know." He pushed back his chair and left the table.

"Chip, come back here and finish your supper," his mother ordered. "I don't know what in the world's got into you lately. You can't talk to your little sister like that. I won't have it."

Chip heard it all, but he kept on going. He was fed up with his family, lonesome for Butch and Joe Kelley, for freedom and a chance to bust loose. He was sick of girls and women, Joanie's giggling and Dolly's snooping and his mother's nagging at him all the time. He ran across the meadow, climbed the hill and sat on a rock, tight as a coiled spring.

Gradually he relaxed. The cool breeze and the quietness, broken only by the sweet song of a wood thrush, made him feel better. His family was all right. If he never heard Joanie's giggle again, he wouldn't care, but it might be fun, at that, to go to the lawn party.

He sat there a long time. In the distance he heard girls' voices. Anger surged through him. If they were chasing him, he'd be jiggered if he'd take them anywhere. The voices came nearer, and Chip thought he was seeing things. He rubbed his eyes and looked again. There were four girls, five, six, seven girls, breaking through the underbrush, all talking at once. One of them was Sharon Tower.

"Chip!" she cried, as astonished as he was. "Oh, Chip, am I glad to see you! We're lost. I was sure I knew the short cut over the hill, but we got in a mess—nothing but briars and fallen trees to climb over. Whew! I'm practically dead. In fact, we all are."

"Where did you come from?" He looked at her tousled hair and the long scratches on her arms.

She pointed to a tall girl, thin as a splinter. "We hitched a ride with Dib's brother. We walked out of

camp right after breakfast for a little excitement. We left a note telling old Bug-eye we'd be back tomorrow."

"You lit out? Ran away? All of you?" Chip asked as one girl after another flopped down on the pine needles and kicked off her shoes.

"Why not? Let her worry. I hope it'll get into the papers. Then she'll flip her lid. Come on, get up," she ordered, and the tired girls struggled to their feet. "Aren't you hungry? You can't sit there all night."

"Where are you going?" Chip asked.

"Home."

"There's nobody there. Your people have gone to Maine."

"I know it, but I know where there is a key. We'll get cleaned up and find something to eat. Then tomorrow we'll hitchhike back to jail." She followed Chip down the winding footpath, the chattering crowd at her heels.

"You're crazy, absolutely nuts," he informed her.

"I like being crazy."

"Then you ought to be happy most of the time," Chip muttered.

At the turn of the trail they met Chip's father. He stood still and stared, as he saw Chip and the gang of girls straggling along behind him.

"What in heaven's name have you got there?" he asked.

"Escapees from the nut house," Sharon told him cheerfully.

"You said it," Chip agreed.

By that time Carol and Joanie had heard the racket, and they came rushing out to see what was going on. They invited the weary wanderers into the house. Chip and his father turned toward the barn.

"I suppose Dolly told you about my room. Do you want to see it?"

"That's up to you."

"Come on." Chip set the ladder in place. After he had opened the windows, he showed his father the contents of the desk, beginning with the lowest drawer, ending with the old stamp book and the letters.

"Some of these stamps are valuable," his father stated. "Have you decided what you're going to do with them?"

"I don't know yet."

His father gave him a long, searching look, but said nothing. He swung around in the swivel chair to inspect the room. "You could fix this place up and have a real den here. I'll help you make a rope ladder that you can haul up after you. Then you can really get away from it all when you want to."

"Thanks, Dad." For a long time they sat there, Chip on the book box, his father at the desk studying the stamps in the brown book.

"Dad, there's something I think I ought to tell you," Chip began.

"Well, this is as good a chance as you'll ever get," his father replied.

"I know I should give those letters and the stamps to Mr. Collins, and I'd be willing to, but . . ." He held the padlock in his fingers and snapped it shut, unlocked it

and clicked it again. He hated to tell his father he had
been wrong about the old man. He wished there were
a way of saying it that wouldn't hurt, but there were
no easy words. "Dad, Mr. Collins gypped you. When he
saw you, he raised his price."

Mr. Wood swung around to face his son. "What makes
you think so?"

"One of the Redfield boys told Freddy Greer." Once
he was started, it was a relief to tell his father the whole
story.

"It may be true, Chip, but I doubt it. The old man
seemed fair and unprejudiced. And Freddy, I'm sorry to
say, is neither. Let's give Mr. Collins the benefit of the
doubt until we have proof."

Chip nodded. He respected his father's judgment. It
was reassuring to know that his faith in the old man
could not be shaken by anything Freddy Greer might
say. "Of course, Mr. Collins might not want the stamps,"
he said slowly.

"That's possible."

"Well, I'll think about it. Where does he live?"

"On Berkley Street, with his son Leonard. He's a
lawyer. I met him the day the papers were passed."

"Oh." Chip gnawed his thumb and looked out the
window. Mr. Collins was a very old man. His son was a
lawyer. Lawyers were rich. The stamps would mean little
or nothing to either of them, but the money they would
bring would make life so much easier for the Woods.

A tremendous racket interrupted his thoughts. He

started to his feet. "Boy, oh boy, Dad! Look what's here! The police car! And isn't that Mr. Tower?"

"It certainly is." The runaway campers were there, too, and Carol and Joanie, and Mrs. Wood and Dolly, all talking loudly and at once.

"Uh oh, looks as though the news reached them fast," Chip said.

"Poor Sharon. She's a mixed-up kid if I ever saw one." Mr. Wood closed the windows as Chip replaced the stamp book and began to lock up. "When you get this place fixed up, I may borrow your key and come here myself, when the women get too thick down below."

"We'll paint a sign: THE DEN. MALE ANIMALS ONLY." Chip chuckled. "Whew, I'm hungry. Do you suppose there's anything left to eat in the house, or did Carol feed those buzzards?"

"Only one way to find out," his father commented. "Let's go," and he followed Chip down the ladder.

CHAPTER NINE

SEPTEMBER

Nothing exciting happened for a long time after that. Chip and his father worked long hours. They were out at six in the morning to cut glads, sweet peas and dahlias for the wholesale trade, and more flowers and vegetables for their own roadside stand under the elm tree, where Carol spent most of her time. The tangle of blackberry bushes had to be cleared for another season; wood had to be cut for the winter woodpile; poison ivy had to be sprayed. There was no end to the work, no limit to their plans and dreams for the future.

What to do with the stamps was still worrying Chip. He often thought of old Mr. Collins, climbing the ladder and sitting in the little room, rereading his son's letters, and then turning to the old stamp book to live again his boyhood days. Chip had very definite ideas of right and wrong, and it was an uncomfortable compromise to keep things that were not one hundred per cent his own. Little by little, the joy of finding the stamps was completely overshadowed by his dissatisfaction with himself. He tried to forget the whole business, but that was not easy. At last he went to his father.

"Dad," he said, "next time you go to Courtney, I want to go with you and find Mr. Collins. I'll ask him if he wants those stamps. I hope he doesn't but, anyway, I'll give him the letters and have a chance to talk with him."

"Good. Whichever way it turns out you'll feel better about it." His smile made Chip feel good. He was sure everything would turn out right. As he packed the letters and stamp book into a carton, with a few town reports on top, he could picture the old man's pleasure in unpacking it. He could almost hear him saying, "Chip, my boy, wouldn't you like to have the stamps for your collection?" And then Chip would be sure that his father had been right and that Mr. Collins was a kind gentleman, and the stamps would be Chip's and no question about it.

However, it didn't turn out that way. When he rang the Collins' bell, a lemon-faced housekeeper told Chip that the family had gone to their home in Provincetown for the summer, and that the old gentleman was asleep. Was there any message?

Chip explained briefly and gave her the box. She took it, said thank you, and closed the door.

"I wish I could have seen him," Chip told his father.

"Well, you did the right thing. Remember the old expression, 'Virtue is its own reward.' "

"I didn't expect any reward, but I wish I could have talked to him. I'd like to know whether those stamps mean anything to him now. Maybe he's so old he can't see. Maybe he's so old he's kind of foolish, and the housekeeper won't even bother to show them to him." They were six blocks nearer home when he added, "I wish I'd never gone there."

"It's done. Forget it."

Mr. Wood had his own worries those days. Considering it was a new venture, the flower business had been good, but money was needed for so many things: more plants, advertising, time-saving machinery, a greenhouse to insure a year round income, a water system.

Chip knew all this. He knew, too, that already there were cool mornings, when the shivers ran down his spine. He hated to think of winter, of bathing and dressing in the unheated bedroom. Before they could have a furnace, they must have more money, and that brought Chip back to the stamps. He wished he'd been born into a family that could use a piece of luck without questioning the right and wrong of everything that happened. He knew plenty of families like that, and nobody ever held it against them.

Sharon came back on Labor Day, full of talk about her weeks in Maine, and what happened to the various girls following their escapade. She was delighted to see the flower gardens again, and she helped Carol at the stand, and brought picture books to read to Dolly.

One evening she joined Chip and his father as they were driving stakes for a tall dahlia.

"I don't like the big, cabbagey ones," she told them, "but I love the little pompoms." She turned to slip her fingers under the tightly quilled blossom of a red cactus variety. "I like this one the best of all. What is its name?"

"That one has no name yet," Mr. Wood told her. "It's one of my seedlings."

"You mean it's a new kind? You can name it anything you want?"

"In time."

"Why not now? How do you do it?"

"By cross-pollination." She listened, her face alight with interest, as Mr. Wood explained how he would mark this plant and divide the tubers in the spring. "There will be little nubs, or sprouts on them, like the sprouts on potatoes. You've seen them."

"Yes."

"Dahlia roots, or tubers, are sometimes called "toes." They divide into separate parts something like knobby toes, and each part that has a sprout on it will grow. So we cut them into pieces, and make three or four or sometimes more new plants from every old one."

"Then next year you will give them a name?"

"No. We must watch each one as it blossoms and wait several years to make sure the flowers don't revert or change color."

Sharon looked at the three long rows of plants which, Chip told her, were all his father's seedlings. "I think your father's a wonderful man," she said.

Mr. Wood smiled, but Sharon went on, "Don't laugh. I'm serious. I think your whole family is tops. I like the way you work together, and everybody is interested in what the others are doing. I wish J. P. would let me stay in Redfield this year and go to high school with Chip and Carol."

Chip picked up another stake and hammered it down with sure, strong blows, while his father tied the plant in place with a stout strip of old sheet.

Suddenly Sharon snapped the lovely flower head from its stem and threw it over her shoulder. "Oh, what's the use?" she said angrily. "They would never give up going to Florida to stay home with me. And they'd die before they'd let me stay with you, even if you'd have me." She turned and walked away.

"Sharon, wait," Mr. Wood called.

"What for?" she asked, without stopping.

They let her go. The following week she went back to her boarding school. Chip and Carol enrolled at Redfield High, an ancient brick building that housed all the grades from seven to twelve. Dolly went by bus to a fine new elementary school at the other end of the town.

Schools were much alike, big or small, Chip decided, sizing up his classmates. They were all here, just as in Courtney—the Brains, the B's, and the Bones. He was going to get with the B's. Carol, with her A's, was too close on his heels to allow for any flunking. It was a fresh start, a new chance. He was determined to make good.

The teachers looked all right, but it took time to find out about them. He had discovered that long ago. Some who looked easy were hard markers. Some would let you fool one day, and the next day land on you like a ton of bricks if you dropped a book purely by accident.

His new English teacher was Miss Dickinson. She looked like somebody's grandmother, fat, with short white hair. She talked to Chip about the D on his card from Courtney High, and told him she'd give him a chance, but if he didn't earn C's at least, he would have to drop back a class. He promised to do his best.

"It's up to you, young man," she said, looking him straight in the eye.

"I know it."

She smiled, and he liked her. He hummed a tune as he walked down the corridor. Of course he couldn't be sure until after the first marking period, but he had a feeling he'd get along all right.

Pat Moore met Chip for lunch, and several of the baseball team joined them at their table. Chip had a warm, happy feeling. He knew he was going to enjoy this funny old high school. He saw Carol with another colored girl at a table nearby, and asked the boys who the other girl was.

"That's Merlene Brown. She's got a brother around here somewhere. She's all right, but he's . . . well, he's not your kind, if you know what I mean," Pat explained.

Chip knew. Of course there were friendly and unfriendly, honest and dishonest, hardworking and lazy people everywhere, regardless of their color. Although he'd been lucky himself, he knew what it was like to be "around somewhere" alone, probably on the outside and not welcome in any group.

"I'd like to say Hello to him," Chip said.

They found him in the back of the lunchroom, and he was alone.

"Hi," Pat said, "this is Chip Wood. They've bought the Collins place on Quaker Hill. This guy's name's Quint Brown. Well, I'll be seeing you." Pat and the others drifted away.

"I heard about you," Quint said. He was a tall, light Negro with sullen eyes.

"I saw your sister with my sister, and I thought I'd say Hello," Chip began, hardly knowing what to say. The other fellow sprawled over the table without saying anything. "What year are you?"

"I dunno. They call me a special. I'm waiting to be sixteen and get out of this dump."

"Do you play on any of the teams?"

"No."

"I thought I'd try for football."

"Aw, they got a lousy team. I played on it last year. They always get beat." He dug at a hole in the table top with the prongs of his fork and his lips curled in a sneer. "Fella told me you're college course. Huh. You crazy?"

"No. Why?"

"What'll it get you?"

"Well, my father went to business college, and I'd like to go to Mass. State after high school. You've got to have a good education to . . ." His voice trailed off before the scorn in Quint's eyes. Chip felt like a good little god in a tin halo talking about education and what it would get you, so he changed the subject. "I wish you'd look us up some time."

Quint picked up his plate and milk bottle and stuck the fork inside. "Aw, I don't fit with college people. I suppose you're the kind that gets all A's without even trying."

"No, but I wish I did."

"Huh. Professor. Wise guy."

The bells buzzed and Chip was glad of a chance to get away.

The next week he made the scrub football team. It was one more reason for liking Redfield High. As the farm work slackened, Chip's father took over, and Chip was soon absorbed in school activities.

It grew steadily colder as September days passed. Chip carried pitchers of hot water to his room, but the chill in the air made bathing uncomfortable. By winter, he was sure, he would never wash at all. The kitchen was always nice and warm, with a good wood fire in the old iron stove. The Miss Morgans loaned them a stove for the living room. It was not as pretty as the open fire, but it heated the room much better. When the family gathered there in the evening, studying or reading, it was comfortable and snug.

The cold bedroom was hardest on Dolly. She had begun school with noisy enthusiasm, but by the end of September she was sick with a cold. From then on she was out of school more than she was in. She soon dropped behind her class, and after that she didn't like school.

It wasn't like her to fuss and cry. They took her to the young Redfield doctor. She didn't like him, and she begged for Dr. Graham, the Courtney doctor they all loved.

The killing frost they had been dreading came early in October, on a clear, still night when the moon was full and all outdoors was almost as bright as day. When the morning sun reached the dahlia fields, the ruin was complete. Wet, black leaves and blossoms filled the fields that had been so colorful and bright.

The end of the growing season meant more work for Chip. The stalks had to be cut, the tubers dug, marked, and packed in cartons, barrels and boxes, and stored in the deep cellar of the house. It was a good cellar, with a dirt floor. Bins of winter apples and vegetables, and shelves filled with Mrs. Wood's canning lined one side. The family wouldn't go hungry.

Chip was so busy writing a book review that would keep Miss Dickinson smiling, studying for a social studies test, singing with the Glee Club, and practicing football passes in hopes of being chosen to substitute in one of the big games, that when his father decided to take his old job at the office in Courtney for the winter, it didn't trouble Chip at all. In fact he was glad. It gave him a comfortable, secure feeling to know that steady money would be coming in again.

Redfield was all right. He liked living there. He wasn't worrying his head one single bit about anything any more.

CHAPTER TEN

THANKSGIVING

Chip was a good sleeper. Once in bed, with three blankets over him and a hot brick to keep his feet warm, he was dead to the world. It took his alarm clock, his mother, and sometimes his father, too, to wake him those cold, dark mornings. So it was strange to wake suddenly at two o'clock in the November night. Why, he wondered. A shutter was rattling. Rain beat against his window, which was open a few inches. He knew he should close it, but he hated to get up.

"Raspberries," he mumbled, slowly pulling his toes from the warmth. When he reached the window, he saw the lights were on downstairs. He stood there, shivering, listening to voices—his father telephoning, his mother asking questions, and Dolly crying and coughing. He knew she had been sleeping on a cot in their bedroom. He felt as though a cold hand were squeezing his throat as he grabbed his bathrobe and hurried down the stairs.

She must be sick, very sick, if they were calling a doctor in the middle of the night.

She lay propped up against the pillows on the little camp cot. Her mother sat beside her, a glass of medicine in her hand. Chip could hear his father smashing ice cubes in the kitchen.

"What's the matter?" Chip asked.

"My ear hurts," Dolly wailed.

"Hush, darling. Don't try to talk. Take your medicine," her mother pleaded. "One more spoonful. That's a good girl."

Chip's teeth were chattering as he went to the kitchen.

"You called the doctor, Dad?"

"Yes. He said to try ice bags instead of heat."

"Is he coming?" Chip trailed his father back to the bedroom.

"He'll be here in the morning."

"Yes, in the morning," Mrs. Wood repeated. "No matter if she has a temperature of 103, he wouldn't come in the night. I wish we'd never left Courtney and come to this God-forsaken place. Dr. Graham would have come. He wouldn't have . . ."

"Sssh, Anna, Dolly'll hear you. If this doctor thinks it's serious, we'll send for Dr. Graham. Here, darling, this'll feel good." He placed the ice bag against her neck. She flinched, but lay still.

Chip reached down and pushed a lock of hair from her hot forehead. He longed to do something to help. He longed to have his family back to normal, not here in the brightly lighted room in the middle of the night:

his mother, with her straight black hair falling to her shoulders and her big black eyes burning with anger and fear, his father, in an old faded bathrobe, his face lined with anxiety.

Rain bubbled up around the window sills. Chip got a rag and mopped it up. Nobody noticed him.

"Don't you think she feels a little better now?" he asked, after wiping all the wet sills.

"Go to bed, Chip," his mother answered. "There's nothing you can do to help."

He went unwillingly, and lay awake until the clock struck five. Then he dressed and went down again. His mother was on the big bed, asleep. His father held Dolly, wrapped in a blanket, in his arms.

That early morning was the beginning of a strange period in Chip's life. Carol made their breakfast, and the young Redfield doctor came while they were trying to eat it. Dolly, he said, should go to the hospital.

"We'll take her to our own hospital in Courtney," Mrs. Wood stated. "Chip, you hold her, while your father and I make arrangements to go."

"I'm afraid," Dolly whispered, as he leaned over her.

"Listen, you'll like it, Dolly. Dr. Graham will be there, and he'll fix you up in no time. There'll be lots of nice nurses, and lots of other little girls, and you'll have things to play with, and Mom's going to stay at Grannie's so she'll be near you all the time." He kept on talking while his father got the car out, and his mother brought warm blankets and shawls to wrap Dolly in.

"Chip, keep the wood box filled and both fires going.

Take the key to the back door, and don't you dare to lose it. Help Carol all you can. You're old enough to get along by yourselves."

"Sure. We'll be all right."

He held Dolly while his mother got into the car, and then they were gone. Chip returned to a strangely empty house. "What do you suppose they'll do to her?" he asked Carol.

"They'll give her penicillin. She'll be all right as soon as she sees Dr. Graham. We've got to hurry, or we'll be late to school. I'll leave the beds and dishes until I get home, and then I'll make a chocolate pudding for supper, the kind Daddy likes."

He looked at her round, placid face as she stacked the dishes in the pan and poured hot water over them. "Aren't you worried?" he asked.

"What good does it do to worry?"

During the days that followed it seemed to Chip she enjoyed being the housekeeper, but for him the clocks stood still. Each day his father visited the hospital; each night he brought home news. Dolly was in an oxygen tent; then she was out of it, breathing better, but the ear infection and the fever continued. Their mother had gone to work in the hospital as a nurses' aide so that she could be near Dolly. The days dragged on.

The Tuesday before Thanksgiving, as they ate more meatballs and jello pudding, Mr. Wood asked, "Do you think you could roast a chicken for Thanksgiving, Carol?"

"I could, but let's wait until they come home. I don't feel like Thanksgiving." Her lips quivered and she began to cry. "I don't see how Mommy ever does all the work here. It's so cold to wash out things, and I freeze my hands when I make the beds upstairs."

"Don't you help her, Chip?" his father asked. "Don't you make your own bed?"

"Sure I do."

"You didn't yesterday or today," Carol said, mopping her eyes.

"Give me time. I'm going to."

"And I'm afraid that when Dolly comes home she'll get sick again. It's so cold everywhere. It's just like going to bed outdoors. Oh, I wish we were back in Courtney." And Carol, who never cried or got upset, laid her head on the table and sobbed as though she would never stop.

Her father patted her shoulder. At last he said, "We should have a furnace. Right away. This winter."

"Can you get another loan from the bank?" Chip asked.

He could almost see his father's thoughts spinning. Even with the Blue Cross insurance, there would be some doctors' bills and hospital bills; and a heating plant this year would postpone the greenhouse another year, or maybe two.

"Perhaps we could get a second-hand one," Chip volunteered.

"We'll see."

"I think I'll have frankfurters and potato salad," Carol said, sitting up and wiping her eyes on a fresh kleenex.

"Okay with me. I don't care what I eat," Chip stated briefly.

Early Thanksgiving morning Sharon telephoned. Inga had told her about Dolly's illness, and she was much concerned.

"I'm going to the hospital with Dad at two o'clock," Chip told her. "I'll call you when I get back."

"Oh, I hope she's better. Ear trouble is serious."

The words echoed through Chip's head as he walked through the long slippery corridors to the children's ward. His mother, trim and cheerful in her blue uniform, met them at the door. As Chip went to the cubicle where Dolly lay, a nurse came in with a box of flowers for her, pink rosebuds and tiny blue iris, and lacy ferns.

"What lovely flowers!" her mother exclaimed. "Who sent them?"

Chip found the card. "Sharon," he said.

His mother's lips closed in a hard, straight line. "So she's home again. Hasn't this family got trouble enough without her? Chip, I don't want her around. Don't let her in the house. She's not a good companion for Carol, or you, either."

"She's just home for Thanksgiving," Mr. Wood explained. "I don't believe she'll contaminate us in that short time."

"I don't like her. She's rude and . . ."

"Mama, I like her," Dolly interrupted. "Tell her the flowers are very pretty."

"All right," Chip answered. "I'll tell her. And I'll tell her you're getting better." He gave her a brotherly pat as they left.

He was glad they had made no promises to Mom,

for when they got home Sharon was there. The dining room table was set with a white cloth and the best dishes, and vegetables were cooking. Sharon was unmolding pink gelatine salads, while Carol cut thick slices of cranberry sauce with a turkey-shaped cutter.

"Is Dolly better? I knew she would be." Sharon plunged into an explanation of what was going on. "We had a turkey as big as an elephant, and as a kindness to the Towers, I brought you what was left. We didn't even cut the second side, and it would have lasted from now till Christmas." She gave Mr. Wood an impish grin. "You should have seen me. I tied the turkey to the silver platter and brought all this stuff over on your wheel-barrow. See!"

She opened the oven door, and there was the bird in all its beautiful golden-brownness.

"You shouldn't have done that, Sharon," Mr. Wood said firmly.

"Why not? If I want to do a kind deed once a year, just once a year, why shouldn't I do it? Carol said you were going to have hot dogs."

"We could have had a chicken if she'd wanted to cook it." Chip looked at Carol's happy face and said no more. A turkey dinner, no matter where it came from, was a welcome change from frankfurters, beans and spaghetti.

It was a festive table. The Tower turkey, good side up, was a noble bird. The vegetables looked and smelled delicious. Chip slid into his chair, his mouth watering in anticipation.

"Shall we bow our heads a minute?" Mr. Wood asked. At their big family dinners, their grandfather always asked a blessing, but Chip hadn't expected it today. And yet, it was a time for Thanksgiving.

"We thank Thee, Heavenly Father, for this food, and for the kind heart of our neighbor, Sharon Tower. Bless us all, and Mother, and Dolly. Amen."

As his father picked up the carving knife, Chip looked at Sharon. She was wiping her eyes and her nose on one of his mother's best linen napkins.

There was no one to make them do the dishes, so when they finished eating they sat a long time at

the table postponing the unpleasant task. Conversation
drifted from the good dinner to Carol's cooking, from
Sharon's school experiences to the less exciting events
at Redfield High. But always it returned to Dolly, and
the wish that they could get a furnace right away, so
that the house would be warm when she came home
from the hospital.

Suddenly Sharon stood up. "What time is it? We're
having company tonight, a girl Jud met, and a couple
of his school friends." She turned to Chip. "One of them
knows you."

"Freddy Greer, I suppose."

She nodded. "He seems awfully nice. Why does he
hate you so?"

"I don't know."

"Oh, but you do," Carol contradicted. "Freddy has
never forgiven Chip for giving him a beating when they
were little boys."

"Why bring that up?" Chip growled.

"Bring what up? I want to know what happened."
Sharon sat down again and planted both elbows on the
table.

"We had a fight once, and I broke his tooth. Nothing
to tell."

"Oh, come on, Chip, it's a better story than that,"
Mr. Wood chuckled. "You see, Sharon, Freddy's two years
older than Chip, but he was always picking on little boys
when he lived on our street. Chip came home day after
day crying, 'Freddy called me names. Freddy hit me.
I knew it would do no good to talk to Freddy's parents

because they were very angry when we bought our house on King Street."

"Freddy lived on the same street you did?" Sharon asked in surprise. "I thought his father had money."

"He's fairly well off."

"He bought Freddy a swell car, cream and blue. It's a keen job," Chip broke in.

"I know. Tom Greer's killing himself trying to keep up with Freddy. I doubt if there's anything that boy ever wanted that his father didn't buy for him. Freddy's the most important member of the family, and that's enough to spoil any boy."

"I never thought of that before," Sharon said slowly. "But what happened to Freddy and Chip?"

"I don't believe in fighting," Mr. Wood explained. "It never settles troubles, particularly for colored people in a white neighborhood. I told Chip he must avoid the children who bothered him, and not get mad if they teased him, because all the people on King Street would be watching us to see how we were going to behave. But the day came when he couldn't take any more from Freddy Greer. He was just a little chap. You were in first grade, weren't you?"

"Second," Chip mumbled.

"Well, anyway, one day Freddy grabbed his cap, and when Chip tried to get it, Freddy twisted his arm. Then, as near as we can make out, Chip shut both eyes and let him have it with his fists, and then fell on top of him, bumping his head on Freddy's mouth. It cut Freddy's lip and knocked out his new front teeth. It took two

teachers and the janitor to separate them. When the
school nurse brought Chip home, my wife almost fainted.
He looked as though he'd gone ten rounds." Mr. Wood
chuckled, remembering. "The playground kids were all
rooting for Chip, and Freddy never got over it."

"That's a cool story." Sharon's eyes were dancing.
"Every time he smiles, I'll look at his teeth. Oh, dear,
we've got to get to work. Mr. Wood, you and Chip
help me. I'll stay long enough to do the dishes and let
Carol rest."

"Okay, I'll help. But it doesn't mean I'm doing the
dishes all the time," Chip told Carol as he pulled out
the dishpan. "I'll wash."

"Rinse them first," Sharon insisted, "and Mr. Wood,
you'd better fill that big pan. We're going to need oodles
of hot water."

They were still working when a loud knock sounded
on the door.

"I expected it," Sharon said, as her father walked in.
He looked at them, at the dishes, and at the mangled
remains of the turkey on the silver platter.

"So this is where you are," he said to Sharon.

"What a remarkable deduction," she answered saucily,
polishing a copper-bottomed saucepan till it shone. Then
her mood changed, and she spoke quietly to her father.
"Please don't say anything to spoil this day. They were
having hot dogs for dinner. Hot dogs on Thanksgiving,
and we had so much more than we needed. I wanted
to share some of it with them."

"So I see," her father said coldly. "Next time please

consult Inga or your mother before you give things away. Of course, it never occurred to you that we might be planning to have cold turkey at the buffet supper tonight."

"The freezer's full of food. But if you've got to have turkey, take it." Her voice grew shrill with anger. "Take it. Take it. There's still a lot of meat on it. You're so selfish. Selfish. Selfish."

"Sharon, that's enough. Quite enough. Get your coat and come with me."

Chip saw tears in her eyes as she pushed past him.

"Here. Take your old turkey. We don't want it." He lifted the heavy platter and held it out towards Mr. Tower.

"No. You are quite welcome to it. It is just that we have guests and Sharon has embarrassed us, both by her unexplained absence and by her thoughtlessness." He turned to Mr. Wood, and Carol, who had come back to the kitchen with Sharon. "I am very sorry to hear of your little daughter's illness. Are you ready, Sharon?"

"Yes, I'm ready," she stormed, "but I'm coming back tomorrow to help Carol make a dress for Dolly, and you can't stop me." He held the door open for her, and they went home.

"She shouldn't have brought the turkey without asking her mother," Carol said.

"No, she shouldn't have done it," Mr. Wood agreed, "but she meant all right, poor little kid." He picked up a dry dish towel. "Carol, you put things away and let's get this job done. It's after eight o'clock. No wonder her father was worried."

When the work was done, Chip went for a walk. It was a beautiful moonlit night, and he went farther than he had intended. Without planning it, he found himself outside the Towers' brightly lighted house. The ship weathervane shone like silver, reminding him of the one he had meant to make. But it was not of the weathervane he was thinking, as he stood in the shadow of a big fir tree and listened to the gay dance music.

Freddy Greer was in there dancing. What strange fate kept bringing him back into Chip's life? And why was it right that he should go to a private school and be invited to parties as a house guest, when he was such a stinker? It wasn't a nice word, but that's exactly what Freddy was. A stinker. Chip's toe tapped out the rhythm of the rock and roll.

Someday, he thought, as he turned to go home, he'd go to dances again. He loved to dance. Suddenly he was homesick for Courtney and the good times he had had there, the dances at school, and the fun in their own living room when the young people from the church met there, and he made up new steps to every record in the pile. That was one thing about Joanie, she could dance.

He walked home slowly in a strange mood of wanting something and not knowing what. When he opened the door, he found his father measuring the dining room walls. On his desk was a paper filled with figures.

"Something tells me the Woods are going to have a furnace," Chip called. "Three cheers!"

"Come here. You, too, Carol. These things have a

direct bearing on your lives, and you're old enough to help make decisions. It isn't an occasion for cheers." He pushed the paper towards them. Furnace, bathroom fittings, hot water tank and heater, kitchen plumbing, cesspools, estimated cost of plumbers, masons, carpenters, electricians. Opposite each item was a sobering figure.

"I think we ought to do it now," he said, looking at their thoughtful faces, "but I want you to realize there won't be any money available for a long time for clothes, or extras like fancy Christmas presents . . . or college."

"Dad, I'll go over to the Morgans' again tomorrow and see if they need me now. They told me to come in a week or so. I'll help all I can," Chip promised.

"I'm old enough to baby-sit nights as well as Saturdays," Carol said. "And I already have your Christmas present started, and Sharon's going to help me make a cute little dress for Dolly from one of her dresses. It's pink linen and . . ."

"All right, Carol," Chip broke in, "a warm house is the best present for Dolly and everybody. We don't appreciate things until we don't have them any more. I can remember when Mom used to have to make me take a shower. Boy! I'd liked to have had one some of those hot days last summer!"

"To get back to Christmas presents," Mr. Wood interrupted, smiling, "I can think of no nicer present for a father than having a son and daughter like you." He looked from Chip to Carol with misty eyes. "As long as families stick together, they come through all right."

"Dad, you said a mouthful," Chip agreed.

CHAPTER ELEVEN

MISTAKE

At ten minutes past eight the following morning, Sharon
Tower rushed into the Woods' kitchen. Her face fell as
she saw the breakfast dishes in the sink. "Oh, your
father's gone," she wailed. "I want to see him. I want
to tell him something. It's utterly, positively terrific. And
I'm sorry about yesterday."

"You mean about the turkey?" Carol asked as she
carried a kettle of hot water from stove to sink. "You
told me your mother knew you were bringing it."

Sharon sighed and shook her head, as she slid out of
her leather jacket and into the kitchen rocker, dangling
one jodhpurred leg over the arm.

"Why do you want to see my dad?" Chip asked, as
he thrust another stick into the stove and banged it down
so the cover would fit.

"Stop the noise and I'll tell you." She shifted her

position so that she could hug both knees. "Now hear this," she announced solemnly. "I have a furnace for the Woods."

"Oh no, you haven't!" Chip exploded. Then, picturing this blond dynamo pushing a wheelbarrow load of furnace to their door, he burst out laughing.

"That's not polite," she scolded. "Pack this in your cerebellum, Chip Wood. I worked on J.P. two hours before his cold heart melted. It's a perfectly legitimate furnace, in a house he owns that's being torn down. J.P. is saving the doors and panelling and stuff, and he says you can have the furnace."

"You mean for nothing?"

"Yes. Just the cost of moving it. And it's a good furnace, Chip."

"My father will pay all it's worth. He wouldn't want to be under any obligation to your father, or to you, either."

"Forget it. It might be months before J.P. could find anybody else who wants it, and they're already tearing the place apart."

"What kind of furnace is it?"

"Is there more than one kind?"

Chip almost said how stupid can you get? But after all, she wasn't his sister. "Steam, hot water, hot air . . ." he began patiently.

"J.P. said there are radiators, and he was talking about an oil tank. Let's go over and give it a look. I know where the house is." In one lithe motion she was at Carol's side, stacking dishes in the wall cupboard. "I'll finish up here."

"I'll get our bikes," Chip said.

"And I'll make the beds first." Carol, the ever con-
scientious housekeeper, disappeared up the stairs.

They found the house without any trouble, a sad old
house, crowded out by the growing town. Several trucks
stood in the driveway, and workmen were going in and
out. Sharon stopped one of them.

"I am Sharon Tower, Judson Tower's daughter," she
said, looking quite a bit like him as she lifted her chin
and gave the man a business-like stare. "My friends and
I are here to look at the furnace in this house."

He started to grin, thought better of it, and removed
his battered hat. "Yes, miss," he said, and stepped aside.
"Go right in. Be careful of loose boards."

They walked from room to room counting the radiators, stepping over piles of pipe and rubble, then made
their way to the basement to look at the green box
that was the furnace, the oil-burning unit, and the huge
tank that rested on wooden horses under the window.

Sharon rapped on it with her knuckles. "You get it
all, the whole works," she chirped. "Isn't it wonderful!"

"It looks all right," Chip admitted, "but it's the part
you can't see that counts." In spite of himself he was
catching her enthusiasm. "My dad knows the different
makes. He'll know what to look for. Can he come in
tonight when he gets home from work?"

They asked the man. He said he was sorry, but they
left at five. However, he assured them in answer to their
questions that the furnace was a good one and had
been heating the house very nicely until the day before

Thanksgiving, when the water was shut off and they started taking out the pipes. He wished he had some use for it. He'd take it quick.

"Chip, ask them to move it to your cellar right now before somebody offers my father some money for it and he changes his mind," Sharon urged. "If you decide you don't want it, you can send it back."

"We ought to wait till our father sees it," Carol argued, running her fingers down the dull, dusty radiators. "I don't think Mom would like these old things."

"They can be painted. I can fix them so they'll look like new." Chip was remembering the figures on his father's estimate of costs. This was the chance of a lifetime. If he waited, they might lose it altogether. Sharon was watching him, her eyes smiling encouragement.

"I'll take it," Chip said.

The workman smiled. "You're a good businessman, young fellow. I can see that. We'll bring it over this afternoon. You sign your name and address here, and Miss Tower, you sign your name, too, just in case your father asks questions."

"Call him up if you have any doubts." She signed in black letters an inch high.

All the afternoon Chip glowed, imagining his father's delight, and wondering how soon the plumbers could come to install it.

"We ought to get things picked up," he said, "so they won't be in the way when the plumbers go to work."

Sharon agreed. Rugs should be rolled up; furniture moved and covered with sheets; curtains taken down.

Carol was horrified. "No," she kept saying. "We should wait."

"Why? I'm here today to help; I can't come tomorrow. Let's get going," Sharon argued.

Chip's enthusiasm held at fever pitch as they worked. True to his word, the workman sent the truck around four o'clock. In no time at all, radiators, pipes, the furnace—everything except the oil tank—was in the cellar. The tank refused to go down the steep stone steps. The men unhinged the bulkhead doors and ripped out part of the sill before they could work it through.

Looking at the damage, Chip felt the first dent in his happiness. They'd never be able to get the thing out again, that was for sure. What if the stuff was junk? It didn't look so good piled up all over the cellar. Maybe he should have waited, and asked his father. As he tried to mend the hinges on the door, the gathering darkness and the cold November wind, and Sharon's contrastingly blithe goodnight as she dashed home for dinner, sent his spirits into a tailspin.

Carol had supper ready at six o'clock, but their father was late that night. It was seven, half-past, nearly eight before they heard wheels crunch on the gravel in the driveway.

"You'd better go out and tell him, before he sees what you've done to the house," she said. "He won't like it, Chip. And Mother won't like it. I told you to wait."

Chip's heart was knocking like a car with six burned

spark plugs, but he got his speech ready: Dad, you see before you a businessman. I've got us a furnace and saved a thousand dollars. He would say it fast and take him down to the cellar. Dad, you see before you a businessman . . .

However, it was his father who got the first word. "Sorry I'm so late, but I've had a day that was a day! I've talked to plumbers and masons, and looked at everything in plumbers' supplies, from chrome faucets to bathtubs. The Woods are going to have a furnace!" He poured hot water into the basin in the sink and began to wash his hands. "Well, aren't you glad?"

"Dad, I'm a furnace . . . a furnace man myself today," Chip began.

"You're a what?"

"I bought a furnace." He gulped and started again. "I mean I didn't buy it, but it's here." He twisted a button on his shirt until it came off, and then looked at it as though he'd never seen a button before.

"What are you saying?"

"Come down to the cellar."

"Daddy, it was all Sharon's fault. I told him not to do it. I told him to wait." Carol's nerves gave way, and she began to drizzle tears.

"In Heaven's name, what are you talking about?"

He soon found out, while the warmed over vegetables and the remains of the Tower turkey dried up in the oven. He was still raging when they sat down to eat. "If it was any good he wouldn't have given it to you for nothing, and anyway, I don't want charity. And I

don't want a hot water furnace with pipes to freeze
every time the electricity happens to go off. We can't
afford to buy oil when we have a woodlot full of wood.
And where will the sideboard go, and the bookcases, and
the desk, with those elephant-sized radiators against every
wall? You must have been out of your mind, Chip, to
have that junk dumped in our cellar."

Chip could think of nothing to say. He had seldom
seen his father so upset. His elation collapsed like a
pricked balloon. He'd been dumb again, and this was
the worst of all his mistakes.

Mr. Wood looked at the slumped shoulders and shook
his head.

"I'm going over to talk to Tower," he said, and went
out alone into the starry night.

CHAPTER TWELVE

DOLLY

Whatever was said at that interview, the outcome was that the Woods kept the furnace. Two hectic weeks followed. A kind-hearted Courtney plumber took his men off a job and came to work for his friend Charlie Wood, so that the house would be warm when Dolly came home from the hospital.

Electric pump, kitchen sink, bathroom and furnace fixtures, plumbers, carpenters and electricians filled the house to overflowing. Mr. Wood stayed home from work to help, and Chip rushed back from school every day to paint radiators, run errands, and clean up. Sometimes he thought the men made plaster dust just to keep him busy, but he was Knight of the Dustpan with no complaints.

Mr. Wood visited the hospital as usual, so that his wife would not suspect what was going on, but in the

113

midst of the muddle the doctor decided Dolly could go home.

"Whew!" Mr. Wood told Chip, "they had me worried. I finally persuaded your mother to go to Grannie's and stay until Friday."

"Dolly's all right?"

"She's fine. Today she was running all over the hospital in her wheel chair. Won't it be good to have her home again!"

There were times that last week when Chip wondered if the happy day would ever come. There were many problems, but the one that concerned him most came the day the plumbers tried to start the furnace. Everything was connected. Two hundred fifty gallons of oil were in the tank. But when they turned the switch, nothing happened.

"Boost the thermostat," Mr. Wood called. Chip rushed upstairs to raise it to 75, 80, 85. The only temperature that went up was his own.

He remembered it afterwards. It was a funny thing about time. A minute can be a minute, a tiny tick of time that goes by like a whizz. At a ball game, or the movies, for instance. A fellow is there two hundred minutes, but they go by so fast it doesn't seem as though there could be sixty ticks in every one. But other minutes are long, dragged-out spaces of time, like the ones when the dentist says to open your mouth, it will be over in a minute. That minute seems to last forever.

The minutes Chip stood watching the electricians and plumbers tinker with the oil burner were like that. He had never fainted in his life, but the dizzy pressure in his head and the sick feeling under his belt buckle made him wonder if he was going to. He watched every move as the men unscrewed pieces and removed them, blew out tubes, assembled the motor again.

He listened as they talked about the thermo-overload, and the stack switch, and all the things that could go wrong with this type of burner, for all the burners that company made had bugs in them, and were very hard to start.

At last it did start, and to Chip the welcome brrrrr that meant heat and happiness was sweet music. For days he kept listening to it, wondering if it shouldn't shut itself off, or if it wasn't time for it to come on again, and what would happen if it didn't.

However, nothing went wrong. It heated the house beautifully. On Friday Chip and his father put the air-tight stove in the shed and opened the fireplace in the living room. Carol loaded the mantel and all the vases with hemlock branches and red alder berries. The house looked beautiful.

Chip and Carol could hardly wait for their father to return from Courtney. They turned the lights on all over the house; Carol checked again and again to make sure everything was ready for supper; Chip kept an eye on the blazing fire in the fireplace. He heard the horn blowing long before the car turned into the drive, and he could picture Dolly leaning over to push it with all her might. He rushed out and took her in his arms, and she clung to his neck and screamed in his ear that she was all better, but she didn't have to go to school until after Christmas if she didn't want to, and she didn't.

Chip led the way into the kitchen. His mother came next, then Carol and his father with the bags. His mother looked at the white sink and gleaming chrome faucets, she smelled woodsmoke and heard the snap and crackle of the open fire. Like someone in a dream she walked into the living room.

"Mama, look!" Dolly wriggled out of Chip's arms and ran to the gleaming radiator. "It's hot, Mama! It's hot!"

Mrs. Wood gave a little cry and put her hand to her mouth. "Oh, oh Charles!" she whispered. He took her in his arms and she burst into tears.

"It's our Christmas present," Chip said, "from everybody to everybody."

"We couldn't have a better one," his mother said, smiling through her tears, "but we'll have a Christmas party, too, the biggest one we've ever had. We'll invite the family and make it a Christmas we'll never forget."

Chip knew they would. They'd get presents somewhere, make them, or earn a little extra money and buy small, inexpensive things. Soon there would be snow to shovel, and now that the furnace was in, he'd have time to do the jobs the Miss Morgans were saving for him. The Woods were over the hump, and nothing could spoil their Christmas. Everything would turn out right. He'd earn a lot of money some way.

He thought about it after he got to bed that night, with the purr of the furnace making sweet music in his ears.

On Sunday evening, while he was wrestling with
Ivanhoe, his English assignment, Dolly came in with
the cards she had received at the hospital. "Chip, look
at my cards," she insisted. "This one is from Joanie, and
this is from Butch, and all these are from Sharon, and
this is from Mrs. Paulson, and Merlene, and Pat Moore,
and Grandma and..."

"Yes, I know, Dolly. They're nice cards." He had
seen them a dozen times already and he only half listened,
because during the last two weeks his school work had
taken an awful beating. He really had to study now.

"And there's something I forgot to tell you," Dolly
went on, leaning across the table. "Mr. Collins was in
the hospital."

That penetrated. "What? You mean the old man who
used to live here?"

"Yes. He was in a wheel chair, and I was in a wheel
chair, and we used to race down the corridor, and I
beat him. He's nice. He told me a secret."

"About the stamps?" Chip asked eagerly.

She shook her head. "No, we didn't talk about stamps,
but he says there's a holly tree on the hill." She stopped
and concentrated, wrinkling her nose and squeezing her
eyes tight shut. "He made me say it three times. It's
over the stone wall near the sycamore tree, and you go
past a big rock...I can't remember any more, but it's
in the woods in a secret place. It's all right to tell you,
though. And the ground is covered with green stuff to
make wreaths, and when he was a little boy he used to
make them and sell them, and Christmas trees, too."

"Well, it's about time you told me. Tomorrow I'll go and look."

"May I go with you?"

"Not until I've found the place. It'll be rough going, all underbrush and briars in there beyond that wall."

The next afternoon he put on heavy boots, took an axe, and started out. As he walked through the field, he heard someone calling. On the road below was Mr. Tower. Chip went down to see what he wanted. The stony expression on his long face showed something was wrong. Well, if it was Sharon, thank goodness she wasn't at their house this time.

"Someone has stolen the weathervane from my garage. Have you any idea where it might be found?" His eyes bored into Chip's with a cold, unblinking glare.

"Me? No. When was it taken?"

"Last night." His lips clamped together and his eyes narrowed. "I know you have always wanted it. In fact, I have seen you loitering around our premises on several occasions."

"Mr. Tower, I never..."

"Thanksgiving night? Have you forgotten how you hung around under our trees? I was watching you to see what you were going to do. You saw me, and went away. Have you forgotten?"

"I was there that night, but I didn't see you, and I only stood there a minute listening to the music." Chip felt his anger getting ready to boil over, but he made an effort to control his voice. "I'm going to make a ship of my own some day, but even if I wasn't, I'd never

steal from you. Not from you or anybody. I'd be ashamed to do anything like that."

Mr. Tower lowered his eyes. "I hope you are telling the truth. The fact remains, however, that the ship is gone."

Chip went on to look for the holly tree, but the joy was gone from the bright afternoon. Boy, he'd hate to have Mr. Tower for a father. It was no wonder Sharon was wacky.

He cut across the dahlia fields and climbed over the wall, following Dolly's directions. The ground cover of creeping Jennie and princess pine was thick and spongy. Chickadees sang to him from the cedar trees. The air had a good piney, woodsy smell. It grew darker as he made his way through a grove of firs, but there at last was the rock. Although the short December afternoon was waning, he couldn't turn back now. He pushed his way through thick underbrush for twenty paces; retraced his steps to the rock and tried a different direction, to the right, to the left, and back and forth again. And then he found it, in a cleared space about forty feet across. He stopped, and felt a tingle run up his spine.

Before him, lit by the last slanting rays of the sun, was the most beautiful holly tree he had ever seen. Its leaves shone as though each one had been varnished, and the varnish scarcely dry. Every twig and branch was bright with clusters of huge red berries. Unconscious of what he was doing, Chip dragged his cap off, and stood there, worshipping the beauty of it.

The cold wind whistling past his ears soon broke the

spell. He walked around the enclosure to see the tree from every side. There was a fortune here! Wreaths trimmed with these holly berries would sell for real money, oh boy, oh boy! No wonder the old man had kept it a secret place. Chip determined he would tell no one except his family. Very carefully he cut one piece to show them, and made his way back through the woods.

CHAPTER THIRTEEN

CHRISTMAS

From then until Christmas, Chip was in the wreath-making business. Inga Paulson, dropping in on her way home as she often did, showed him how to bend wire coat hangers for frames, and how to cover them with moss and ground pine, hemlock or spruce, and add the sprigs of holly for a touch of color. The wreaths sold faster than he could make them, so everybody pitched in and helped, even Dolly, who could untangle the long trailers of creeping Jennie, and bring scissors or twine to the person who needed them.

Those were happy days, and they flew by faster and faster. School was bubbling with holiday doings, a pageant, a party in the lunchroom. At home, plans for the family celebration kept Carol and her mother whispering and hiding things, while Dolly danced through the days like a little queen.

Chip's presents were soon taken care of. He gave
Carol three dollars towards gifts for the grandparents,
Aunt Molly and Uncle Frank and the four little cousins.
She and Dolly could roam the Five and Ten and have
a whale of a time doing the buying. He did his own
shopping in Courtney in half an hour: perfume for his
mother, a tie for his dad, a book about birds for Carol,
and a bear that walked down a board for Dolly. A box
of Christmas cards, and he was through. Why people
made such a fuss over shopping was something he
couldn't understand.

Sharon's vacation began a few days before the high
school closed, and she helped with the wreaths. As she
went with them to gather more greens, Chip showed her
the holly tree. She understood the need of keeping it a
secret, and she promised not to tell.

"We ought to take a piece of holly to Mr. Collins,"
Chip said one night, as they were cleaning up the kitchen.

"That's a good idea," his mother agreed, "and I'll
send him a box of my walnut crisps."

"We'll be going to the Christmas Eve service," Mr.
Wood said. "We can stop on the way in."

They telephoned and found that the old gentleman
was back at his son's home, and they stopped as planned,
on their way to church. Chip rang the bell. This time
the housekeeper asked him to come in. He followed her
into a big bedroom, where the old man, looking as dried
up as a brown leaf, was packed into a wheel chair. His
bathrobe and blankets wedged him in so tightly that he
could have been turned upside down without falling out.

"Come here, Chip," he said, his keen eyes brightening as he saw Chip's straight shoulders and friendly smile. "According to your little sister, you're a fellow worth knowing."

"You can't believe everything Dolly says," Chip said with a laugh. "Thanks for telling us about the holly. I brought you a piece, and some of my mother's cookies." He laid the box on the table and passed the holly branch to Mr. Collins. "It's the most beautiful tree I've ever seen. My father showed me how to clip the pieces without hurting it or spoiling the shape."

Mr. Collins didn't appear to be listening. "Is your family out there?" he asked. "That little Dolly? Yes? Bring them in, the whole kit and kaboodle. I want to see them all."

Chip was proud of his family as they came trooping in. Dolly at once climbed onto the wheel chair and gave Mr. Collins her loudest kiss. Mr. and Mrs. Wood shook hands, pleased to see him again. Chip introduced Carol, who smiled shyly.

The old man looked from one to another. "You all look alike. As nice a looking family as I ever hope to see." He smiled and they smiled. "It does my old eyes good to see you, to know a nice family like you are living on the old place."

He coughed behind his hand and turned to Chip. "I should have thanked you long ago for bringing those letters from my boy. Somehow in the confusion of selling off my things, they were forgotten. My son was going out to get them but he never got around to it. I can't

tell you how glad I am to have them back, and the old stamp book, too. Some of those stamps are valuable. I take it you don't collect stamps yourself."

"Yes, I do," Chip answered quickly. "I know they're valuable. I looked them up in my catalogue."

"I started that collection when I was a little shaver." The old man's eyes took on a far away look. He began a long rambling story that went from stamps to the people who had saved them for him, and then left stamps entirely for tales of his boyhood on the farm.

Finally Mrs. Wood interrupted. "I'm sorry," she said gently, laying her hand on his arm, "but we're on our way to the seven o'clock service at church. We must go, or we'll be late."

After the goodbyes were said, and they were getting into the car, they missed Dolly. Chip went back for her just as she came dancing out the door.

"Where'd you go?" he asked, as she grabbed his hand and hopped down the steps on one foot.

"I forgot to tell him we had a new bathroom with a shower in the tub. He was glad. He's coming to see it just as soon as he gets better."

"Good. I'd like to have him come and see us. He's a fine old gentleman," Mr. Wood said, as he started the motor. "Don't you feel you can trust him, Chip, now that you've seen him?"

"Yes, I do."

Soon they arrived at the candle-lighted church, to greet old friends whom they had not seen since leaving Courtney. Oh, it was good to get back! Chip grinned as

Joanie squeezed into the pew between him and Carol, as she always had.

Joanie was growing up, growing pretty, too. Chip seldom noticed clothes, but he liked her red hood with the fluffy tassel on the top. He kept looking at it, and the dark curve of her cheek. It was good to stand beside her again, and sing with a church full of people who loved to sing, and to hear their kind old minister read the Christmas story. Still, Chip's thoughts wandered back to Mr. Collins. Those stamps didn't seem to mean a thing to him.

Chip sighed. Once Christmas was over, the Woods would have to face it. There would be bills that Blue Cross insurance would not cover, and all the new things in the house had to be paid for. If anybody could use an extra thousand dollars, they sure could.

But worries and Christmas didn't mix. He forgot them all when, after church, they loaded Grandmother and Grandfather, and baskets of food, and a dozen mysterious packages into the station wagon. Aunt Molly and Uncle Frank and the cousins followed in their Chevrolet.

From the minute they got home, the house was full of Christmas. Lights shone from every window. Good smells came from the kitchen, where the women fried hamburgers and bacon for sandwiches, and made coffee. While they worked, Chip sat by the fire with the men. The children romped from room to room, always returning to gaze up at the big tree with its splendid decorations, and the many small packages tied to its branches and the pile of big presents underneath.

During one of the quieter moments, Chip heard someone at the front door. He found Sharon standing there,
her arms full of beautifully wrapped gifts.

"Where's Carol?" she asked. "I've brought some things
for your family." She looked past him to the tree and
the children. "This big box is ... guess what?" She held
it up, as the curious cousins, led by Dolly, came crowding around.

"Candy!" they roared.

"It's for you, all of you. The other packages are for
the Woods."

"Come in," Dolly urged.

"Yes, come in," Carol repeated. "I have a package
for you upstairs. I had to hide it from these little mon-
sters." She smiled at them as they tore the bright paper
and ribbons from the candy box. "All right, now. You
may each have one piece. No more until after supper."

"Candy, candy, candy," they shouted, pulling Sharon
into the dining room to see the table with its gay paper
tablecloth, red candles, and large vase of holly and spruce.

Sharon admired everything, then nestled down on the
window seat, with her arms around Dolly and a twin-
sized cousin. "I know a Christmas story about a little
elf. Inga Paulson used to tell it to me when I was a
little girl. Want to hear it?"

They did, and Sharon held them spellbound as she
described Tomte, the Swedish elf who comes on Christmas
Eve. She looked into their wondering faces as they listened
to every word.

"And if you leave a bowl of milk on the doorstep

tonight, he'll come and drink it all up, and it will make him very, very happy. And then he'll help you all next year."

"Did you give him some milk?" Dolly asked.

"Yes, and in the morning it was gone."

"Oh, I'm going to put some out for him tonight before I go to bed," Dolly declared.

Sharon looked up to see a plump, white-haired woman watching them from the doorway.

"Grandma, this is Sharon," Dolly cried, grabbing her around the knees. "She knows Tomte. May we put out a bowl of milk for him so he will find it if he comes tonight?"

"Of course. All kinds of magical things happen on Christmas Eve." She smiled at Sharon. "I can see that you like children. Have you any little brothers or sisters?"

"No. I wish I had."

"Oh, hello, Sharon," Mrs. Wood said briefly, as she lighted the candles.

"May Sharon stay to supper with us? Mama, may Sharon stay?" Dolly tugged at her mother's apron.

"That's a good idea," the grandmother said. "Nobody is ever turned away on Christmas Eve, and I noticed as I set the table that there are thirteen places. Say what you will, it's an unlucky number."

"Nonsense," Mrs. Wood declared.

"Please stay," Dolly insisted.

Chip, watching from the doorway, saw his mother's mouth tighten. "You may stay, Sharon, if your parents are willing."

"They aren't home." She saw the pitying look on the

grandmother's face, and went on, "Nobody's home. Jud is spending Christmas with a fraternity brother. They're having some kind of initiation stunts during the holidays. J. P. and the Queen are in Boston, and they may wait to hear the carollers and bell ringers on Beacon Hill. So I'd love to stay."

A place was set for Sharon. Fourteen sat down at the long table and bowed reverent heads, while the grandfather asked God to bless them and take care of them through the coming year. Fourteen ate hamburgers and cheese and bacon sandwiches and potato salad and doughnuts until they could eat no more.

Many hands made light work of the dishes. Dolly and the cousins left the bowl of milk for Tomte on the lowest step. Then they went back to the tree to guess again what was in each package, and what Santa would leave in the five red stockings that hung by the fireplace.

"They're staying all night," Carol explained to Sharon, "so we won't open our presents until tomorrow morning. But we always sing carols on Christmas Eve. Don't you want to stay and sing with us?"

"I'll stay, but I can't sing," Sharon replied.

For more than an hour she listened. They sang hymns and Christmas carols, Negro spirituals, White Christmas, Rudolph the Red-nosed Reindeer, any song anyone called for they all knew and sang in beautiful four-part harmony. Sharon, quiet for once, looked from one face to another. Chip wondered what she was thinking.

They were singing "Deck the Halls" for the second time, because even the littlest children could join in the tra la la's, when the door opened, and Mr. Tower walked in. "Pardon the intrusion," he said, "but I knocked several times without being heard. I see my daughter is here, and not at her grandmother's."

All eyes turned to Sharon, whose face slowly turned crimson.

"So what?" she said, defiantly.

"Come home," he answered quietly.

"Merry Christmas," Dolly called, but it didn't seem to fit. The others said good night, as Sharon threw on her coat and left.

"She's a problem child," Mrs. Wood explained, "and unless we're going to have a house full of the same tomorrow, we'd better pack these youngsters off to bed."

That was fun, too, for they let the grownups have the beds, and the children lay on the floor on bed quilts or in sleeping bags. There was a lot of giggling and whispering and tickling each other before they fell asleep.

Chip stayed up with the adults, half listening to their conversation, but mostly thinking about the people he'd seen that day: Mr. Collins, and Joanie, in her pretty little red hood, her bronze skin as smooth as satin, and her eyes sparkling.

He thought of Sharon, too. They would not see her again during the holidays, and he was glad of it. She needn't have been alone on Christmas Eve. She had it all planned to horn in on their Christmas party, coming just at supper time with those presents. Well, if she came out of curiosity, to see what colored people did on Christmas Eve, she had probably learned something.

He looked at the thoughtful, earnest faces of his grandmother and grandfather, aunt and uncle as they discussed with his parents the problems that most concerned them.

"I've lived a long time," his grandmother was saying. "I can see it. Things are a lot better. It's pretty slow sometimes, but we're kind of journeying on up all the time."

"It's like that with races and countries, and individual men and women. Or it ought to be," Chip's father said slowly, his eyes on the fire where a log had fallen apart in a new burst of flame. "It's like a ladder to the sky. The spaces between the rungs aren't even. Sometimes you seem to go fast, and sometimes slow."

Chip's grandfather straightened his bent shoulders. "And some of the rungs aren't even safe to hold your weight," he said, "and others are troubles you have to step on hard to get on up, and so too many people quit, and stay on a low place and stop trying."

Chip grew drowsy as they talked on and on. But before he went to his room to find his sleeping bag, he went outdoors to make sure Tomte's bowl would be empty when Dolly found it in the morning.

CHAPTER FOURTEEN

JANUARY

It snowed after Christmas as Chip had hoped it would, a quiet storm with big flakes that clung to every twig and turned the telephone wires into long white ribbons.

All morning he cleared out driveways. When he could find no more customers, he finished work on a sled he was building to haul down the wood they had cut on the hillside. It was a perfect day, and he was glad to stay outdoors. All afternoon he brought down load after load. Later he would saw it into the right length for stove and fireplace, and they would have a first-class woodpile to last all winter.

The next day he went to Courtney and stayed overnight with Butch. They had a good time going to the movies, bowling with the boys, and watching television, which was a treat for Chip. When he returned to Redfield,

it took him a couple of days to get over being homesick
for the city.

Vacation was flying by too fast. Chip knew he ought
to study. Before Christmas he had let his lessons slide
again. But who wanted to stay in the house and study
during the holidays? Certainly he didn't. Although most
of the snow had melted, he decided to take his sled and
get a few more loads of wood.

It was a cloudy day, warm for December, and so
quiet that when he heard a loud whack and then
another, and another, in the woods on his right, he
stopped and listened, and then went on. It sounded
near, but it must come from the other side of the hill.

The road into the woods was trampled by his coming
and going. He could see the prints of Dolly's feet, where
she had gone with him on some of his trips. Watching
for her footprints, he saw another boot mark. It was
as large as his own, but not his; his boots left a wavy
mark, and this print had diamond shaped corrugations.
That was funny. He looked for more, and found them.
They turned off at the sycamore tree and began again
beyond the wall.

Chip dropped his sled and leaped over. The snow
was trampled in every direction by someone apparently
unsure of where he was going. Chip went to the big
rock and found the prints again. He stopped and listened,
his heart pounding so he shook, his thoughts bouncing
from rock to holly tree, to someone chopping. But who
would want holly after Christmas? And who knew the
tree was there?

The friendly chickadees saw him and called the news back and forth from pine to hemlock as Chip crept along, inching his way toward the clearing. A twig cracked under his foot, and he stood motionless for a minute, listening. Another light blow of the axe set his blood on fire, and he saw red as he came out from behind the last clump of junipers. For there was his holly tree, a dozen of its branches lying on the ground, hacked off, and kneeling beside them, trying to tie them together, was a redheaded boy.

Something snapped inside Chip's head. "What do you think you're doing, you, you, you..." he yelled. If he saw red before, he saw all colors of the rainbow as he recognized Freddy Greer. The axe was between them. Chip made a dash for it and flung it into the bushes, then turned to face his old enemy.

"Well, if it isn't Dahlia Boy," Freddy sneered, standing up, "and he's so mad he's ready to bust."

Chip didn't trust himself to talk, but the glint in his eyes and the tightening of his jaw were not lost on Freddy. "Okay," he said, "if you want to fight, come on and see who gets his teeth knocked out this time."

Chip saved his breath. Freddy was older and heavier, but Chip's muscles were hard and strong, and Freddy's peevish grudge was nothing compared to the hot anger that burned in Chip's heart. He knew he'd win. He had to.

The fight was hot and furious, but it was soon over. Chip had Freddy on the ground, face down among the scattered holly branches, his wrists tied behind him with his own rope.

"Get up," Chip roared, watching with joyous satisfaction as Freddy thrashed around, trying to get a foothold in the slippery snow.

"I'll get even with you. You wait," Freddy threatened, sitting up, legs doubled under him, trying to get enough spring to stand. "You can't do this to me and get away with it."

"Says who?" A long branch loaded with berries lay at Chip's feet. Freddy had chopped off the lower twigs so that he could tie the rope around it. It was too great a temptation; it seemed to lie there begging Chip to use it. He picked it up, looked at it, and at the mutilated tree.

"Says who?" he repeated, and jammed the branch down the neck of Freddy's coat. It caught on the lining. Chip pushed harder, until the stick was out of sight and Freddy's face was framed with prickly holly leaves. "Wear that home, and the next time you go stealing holly, try some other place." Chip jerked him to his feet and started him along the trail.

"Have a heart, Chip," Freddy begged. "It's scraping the skin off my back. I'm bleeding. I know I'm bleeding."

Chip wasn't listening. "Where are you going?" he asked.

"Home. My car's up the road."

"What did you want the holly for?" Chip waited for Freddy to get over the stone wall.

"That's my business."

"Oh? I won't untie your hands until you tell." They crossed the last fields and turned into the road without speaking. "Why did you do it?" Chip repeated, as they reached Freddy's car.

"To get your goat."

Chip yanked the holly branch out. "Sharon told you?"

"Nobody told me."

"Do you expect me to believe that?" Chip had his knife out ready to cut the rope, but he waited.

"It's the truth. I saw you selling wreaths, and I knew you must have a lot of holly."

"And you walked straight to the sycamore tree and over the wall. What a brain the boy must have! Too bad you never use it." Chip put the knife back in his pocket and started to walk away.

"Okay. Have it your own way. Sharon told me."

"Why didn't you say so? I knew it anyway. That's the only way you could have found out." Chip freed Freddy's chafed wrists, and picked up what was left of the holly.

"Can I have that?" Freddy asked.

"What? The holly?" Chip threw it into the back of the car. "Sure. Keep it to remember me by."

"I'll remember you all right." He swung his car around and drove off.

So Sharon had told. Chip felt sick as he walked down the road toward his driveway. How could anybody be like that, pretending to like them and helping them make wreaths, and then go and tell Freddy Greer about the holly tree? She was spending the remaining holidays with her roommate, but some day he'd show her the tree and let her see the damage done because she talked too much. And how Freddy must hate him to do a thing like that. Chip kept thinking about it for days.

And then the old year ended and the new year began. Chip returned to school ready for work. He really studied, pencil in hand, concentrating and testing himself to see if he could remember what he read. He got along well with all his teachers, and he was looking forward to a report card he could be proud of.

He liked everything about that high school. He made one of the basketball teams and soon became its star, and he got Quint to join up again. One night he invited him and Merlene to supper. The girls had a good time playing games all evening, but Quint refused to play. He sat by the fire, unhappy and ill at ease, smoking one cigarette after another. Mr. Wood and Chip talked about cars, horses, movies, gangsters, and sports, trying to find something he was interested in. Quint said, "Yuh?" or nothing at all.

"What do you expect to do when you leave school?" Mr. Wood asked.

Quint shrugged his shoulders and threw his butt into the fire. "I dunno."

A burst of laughter came from across the room where the girls were playing rummy. "I'm out," Dolly shrieked, "and look at all the cards Merlene has left!"

Chip went over to see. Merlene was smiling, but she was a limp, lifeless kind of girl, no sparkle, no zip. She wasn't like Joanie. He couldn't seem to forget Joanie and how different she'd looked that night in church.

Chip started to go back, but Quint was talking fast and low, looking into the fire and pouring it out, and Mr. Wood was shaking his head as he listened. Chip heard him say, "No, Quint, I don't agree. We have the greatest opportunity right here and now that we ever had. It's up to folks like us, every colored man and boy, to prove that we, as individuals, are worthy of respect. It will take time, and patience, and courage."

Chip sat down at the girls' table and they dealt him a hand. His father could help Quint if anybody could. He was sure of that.

Those long winter evenings were crowded with things to be done. Sometimes Chip studied in his own room, but oftener he brought his work downstairs to be with the family. He and Carol helped their father with the catalogue he was working on, to advertise their flower fields, discussing the costs of printing and cuts and covers, and writing descriptions of the different varieties of dahlias and gladioli. Many times in the weeks that followed, Chip looked back on those evenings as the happiest in his life.

They still had things to worry them. They owed money. Nobody had any new winter clothes. Their mother squeezed every penny in the food budget. They didn't go anywhere. And yet they were happy. Chip's restlessness was gone. His family was all right. School was all right. January was a good month.

CHAPTER FIFTEEN

FEBRUARY

February brought the first real blizzard. It began around noon, with soft, light, fast-falling snow which a howling wind whipped into drifts as it fell, leaving a field bare in one place and heaping piles that covered fences and walls in another. When Chip's father came home, the station wagon looked like a house of snow.

"Is it pretty bad?" Chip asked, brushing off the windows and fenders.

"No, the plows are out everywhere. I got held up by a stalled truck. Boy, I'm glad to get home!" Together they closed the barn door and went to the house, where everything was warm and snug and safe from the storm. The wind plastered the windows with snow, and piled up drifts around the sills. It rattled the doors and howled in the chimney, but who cared? It made the house seem more comfortable, and the hot fish chowder and raised biscuits more delicious.

After that there was more snow, off and on, almost every day. Chip had never realized the world could be so beautiful. Snowplows kept their roads cleared, and Chip earned good money digging out driveways. There was good coasting, too, and they swept the snow from a little pond for skating.

Term marks were in, and Chip's were good: B in English; B in Social; A's in math, science and manual arts. It was the best card he had ever had, and all the world looked bright. The days were getting notice-ably longer; the flower catalogue was at the printer's. Boy, Chip thought as he woke each morning. This is the life!

The third Friday in February, he was bringing in wood for the kitchen stove when the telephone rang. It was Sharon, calling from Courtney. She asked for Carol.

"She's out coasting with Dolly," he told her.

"Don't call her. I got this far with Dib and her brother. Can I ride out tonight with your father? Can you get him at the office and tell him?"

"What do you mean? Your folks aren't back from Florida."

"I know that. I'll stay with my grandmother. Tell your father I'll be in the drug store at Rand's Corner, and I'll wait there till he comes. Okay?"

"Okay." Chip hung up. Trouble, always trouble when she showed up. Anyhow, he'd show her the holly tree, and let her see the damage she'd done by talking too much. Perhaps she could lie her way out of that, but he doubted it. He called the office in Courtney and left the message for his father.

When he went outdoors, he met the family coming in. The girls were glad to hear that Sharon was coming, but their mother stated in no uncertain terms that she hoped she'd stay put at her grandmother's and leave them alone.

The rain that had driven them in kept up for an hour, gradually turning to sleet as the thermometer dropped. When Chip went out again he found the top step as smooth as glass; even the gravel walk was slippery. He grabbed the fence just as his feet slid out from under him.

He turned to see his father driving in. "You're home early, Dad," he said. "Did you meet Sharon all right? She's got more nerve than a brass monkey, but I knew you could go by Rand's Corner, and her grandmother's house is on the way, so it wouldn't be much trouble to pick her up."

His father flicked off the lights and got out. "What are you talking about? I haven't seen Sharon."

"Didn't they tell you? Didn't they give you the message?"

"Nobody gave me any message. Where is she?"

"Rand's Corner."

"I hate to take the car out again. They let us go early because the radio warned about icy driving. But I suppose we'll have to get her if you told her we would."

"Charles, you're not going out again tonight." His

wife, a coat thrown over her shoulders, and icy raindrops sparkling on her cheeks and hair, rushed into the barn. "Listen, it's dangerous driving. and that girl can take care of herself. We're not responsible for her. Let her take a taxi to her grandmother's."

"I don't know where she'd find a taxi on a night like this. We've got good tires. It's no worse than lots of nights. It won't take long."

"About six miles?" Chip asked, as he lifted another pail of sand into the back of the car, just in case they should get stuck.

His mother brushed past him and faced her husband. "Charles, please don't go. I'm ... I'm afraid. I've got a feeling ... If it were necessary, all right, I'd say to go, but it isn't necessary." She pressed her hand to lips that trembled.

"Listen, dear, what if it were Carol who was out there waiting?"

"But it isn't Carol. It's Sharon, and she's a spoiled, selfish brat—"

"No, Anna," her husband broke in, "Sharon has plenty of faults, but she isn't a brat. She has tried hard to be friends with all of us. She likes us; in some ways she depends on us. I think we've helped her. And I think I can help her now. That's why I'm going." He leaned out and brushed his lips across his wife's cheek, then slowly backed the car out of the barn.

They skidded as they turned into Quaker Hill Road, but from there on the traction was better, although water on the ice made it necessary to go slowly. When cars passed, Chip held his breath. If one skidded or stopped suddenly, anything could happen.

They were safely down the hill and out of Redfield, turning into the narrow stretch that led to Rand's Corner, when a boy on skates, pulling another boy on a sled that slatted and slewed, completely out of control, suddenly appeared in front of them in the middle of the road, coming too fast to stop.

Chip's father touched the brakes gently, down and up, down, more firmly. It was enough on the icy, high-crowned road. The car slid sideways and down, off the road, down into a ditch to crash against something. Chip heard a loud scream, and voices. Then everything was quiet, and dark, and stayed that way for a long, long time.

CHAPTER SIXTEEN

TROUBLE

When Chip regained consciousness it took a while to remember what had happened. Where was he? It wasn't his room, or his bed. His head weighed a ton. It hurt to turn it on the pillow. A little groaning noise came from somewhere. Maybe he made it, for a nurse in a white uniform was bending over him.

"How's the boy?" she asked.

"All right." His tongue tasted funny, and he ached all over. "Ouch," he whimpered as he moved his legs. "What's the matter with me?"

"You got a bump on your noddle." She stuck a glass tube in his mouth, lifted his wrist, and looked at her watch.

Wrapping his tongue around the thermometer, Chip asked, "Is my father all right?"

"He will be. Bye and bye."

"Is he here? Can I see him?"

"You can't see anybody yet." She wrote on the chart, and smiled at him. "I'll be back in a few minutes with food. Food, boy, food! How does that sound?"

"Good." He closed his eyes.

When he opened them, Dr. Graham was beside his bed.

"I want to see my dad," Chip told him.

"A little later. We'll get you straightened out first." The doctor rolled back Chip's sleeve and swabbed his arm with alcohol, then jabbed in a needle that hurt like a hornet's sting.

"Is he home? He wasn't hurt was he?" Chip persisted. He stretched his neck to watch, as the doctor and nurse put fresh dressings on a gash in his bruised and swollen leg.

The doctor unwound a strip of adhesive tape, and stuck it to the glass table top, before he answered. "He's got some smashed ribs, Chip, and a bad left knee. He's darned uncomfortable, but he'll come along all right."

"Where's my mother?"

"She's with him. They took him to a hospital in Boston where they have special equipment to fix him up. She went with him in the ambulance."

"Where are the girls?"

"At your grandmother's. Everything's going to be all right. There's nothing for you to worry about." He gave Chip's shoulder a friendly pat and went away.

Three days later Chip went home. His mother put her arms around him and kissed him.

"I'm sorry, Mom ..." he began, looking at her tired, sad face.

"It's not your fault, Chip. I thank God you're alive, and I pray every minute your father will be able to walk again. Oh, Chip." She buried her face in his shoulder, her body shaking with sobs, while he looked at the stricken faces of his sisters.

In time his other questions were answered. The station wagon was wrecked. The boys who caused the accident were not hurt. Sharon, after waiting a while, thumbed a ride to Redfield.

"She came to see us at Grandma's. Jud and Freddy were with her, in Freddy's car," Carol told him. "And Mom told her to go away, and stay away, and never come back."

"And Sharon was crying," Dolly added. "Her face was all swelled up, and she was crying like anything."

"Maybe it'll teach her a lesson." Still, he felt sorry for Sharon. He knew how much she liked his father, and oh how she must wish she'd never asked him to stop at Rand's Corner. No wonder she cried.

On Monday he went back to school, his leg still bandaged. Everybody crowded around to ask about the accident and to express their sympathy. It helped to know they cared.

On Sunday Uncle Frank took Mrs. Wood to Boston. No one under sixteen could visit that hospital, so Chip stayed home with the girls. It was a long, anxious day. "When is Daddy coming home?" Dolly kept asking. Late that night, after the girls had gone to bed, Chip asked

his mother the same question. Something was wrong, he knew.

"I don't know when he'll be home. They've taken more X-rays. The doctor calls it a fractured patella. That means knee cap. They've wired it together. He's still in traction, with a heavy weight on his leg to hold it straight. It's awful." She stopped to wipe her eyes. "Don't tell the girls, but I'm afraid he'll never walk again."

"I won't say anything." Chip stared at the dying fire. His dad on crutches or in a wheel chair for the rest of his life. It was too horrible. It couldn't be true. And the hidden meaning in his mother's words, "Don't tell the girls." They were still children, but now he was the man of the family. Never had he felt so helpless.

"Dr. Graham said he would get better." Chip poked the log, and a few bright sparks glowed along the edge of it.

His mother put her hand on his shoulder as he knelt there. "You're like your father, Chip, always looking for the bright side. We can only hope Dr. Graham is right."

The big snow of the winter came that week. It began on Monday, in the night. Tuesday morning the radio warned of falling temperatures, zero, or below. Chip could believe it as he made a footpath to the road. His leg ached with the cold; the wind penetrated his heavy sweater and jacket; it numbed his fingers, even though he wore his father's heaviest mittens.

There was school that day, but it was hard for Chip to keep his mind on his lessons. When word came that they would be dismissed at noon, his heart sank.

"What's the matter?" the girl in the next seat asked. "I hope it will keep up for a week."

"I've seen enough winter for one year," Chip replied.

Chip's math teacher, Mr. Mahler, offered him a ride home. Chip was grateful, for although it wasn't far, walking in the snow was hard on his leg.

"It's blowing rather than snowing," Mr. Mahler said, "but with this wind and the temperature falling, we'll have the coldest night of the winter." They drove up the snowy hill past boys with their coat collars pulled up around their ears, and girls running backwards against the freezing wind.

As they turned into Stonybrook Lane, Chip could see that the snowplows had pushed an enormous pile of snow across his driveway.

"It looks as though I'd better get busy with the shovel before Dolly's bus gets here," he said. "Thanks for the ride."

"Have you got two shovels? I'll help."

That's the kind of teachers they had in Redfield, Chip thought, a warm glow around his heart. It was fun digging the path that day, even though the wind was cold, and it gave Chip a lift to ask his teacher into the kitchen for hot cocoa and doughnuts. Mr. Mahler was a prince! That evening, after extra wood was in and everything securely locked, Chip wrote his father a long letter, and then studied algebra for a solid hour without thinking about the storm.

At bedtime the thermometer stood at zero. Chip shivered, but the radiators were piping hot, and although the wind drove sleet against the windows, the whole house was snug and warm. He went to bed early, and was asleep in five minutes.

It took a long time to wake up, to realize his mother was shaking his shoulder and standing over him with a flashlight.

"Chip, wake up. You've got to help me. The electricity's gone, and the bulkhead door has blown in, and the cellar's full of snow."

He was awake then, shivering so he could hardly pull on his trousers; his fingers so clumsy he couldn't tie his shoes. When he opened the cellar door, a blast of cold air almost knocked him off his feet. He got the snow shovel, pulled on coat and boots, and started down the stairs, his mother following with the light.

Under the weight of the snow, the bulkhead door had broken from the sill, and one end sagged down onto the stairs. They were covered with snow, and a narrow drift like a huge pointed finger extended half way across the cellar floor. Chip pushed, but the door was too heavy to move.

"I'll have to go out and nail something over it," he said.

"No. You mustn't go out. You'd freeze."

But he was already looking for hammer and nails and his canvas pup tent, hoping it would be wide enough to cover the gap.

The snow had stopped, and he made a path by moonlight and nailed the canvas in place.

His mother had hot malted milk ready when he came

in. Before he drank it, he took the thermometer to the cellar.

"Why did you do that?" his mother asked.

"If it's down to freezing, we'll have to start moving things." Yes, the many jars of blueberries, beans, corn, tomatoes; the jams and jellies his mother and Carol had made; the gladioli bulbs, the dahlias, the precious seedlings, the cartons, the barrels. . . .

"Go back to bed now," his mother said, "and try to get to sleep again. It's four o'clock already."

"I'll look at the thermometer first."

"You mustn't go up and down those stairs on your sore leg. The electricity will come on before anything freezes," his mother said firmly, "and even if it doesn't we can all work and move the things in the morning."

"That may be too late," Chip insisted stubbornly. "Those canned things are heavy. It'll take a long time to move them all. And if the bulbs freeze, we'll be out of business. The only safe way is to start now."

"There, I told you. The lights are on again," his mother said.

Like statues they stood there, listening. Yes, the lights were on. The refrigerator began to hum reassuringly. But from the basement came no sound except the vicious wind tugging at the cellar door.

CHAPTER SEVENTEEN

DISASTER

Chip took no credit for being better than other boys. He often pretended to study when he wasn't studying at all; he got out of doing unpleasant tasks by forgetting them, or leaving them for Carol; he argued and fussed like all teen-agers. But he didn't deliberately and defiantly disobey his mother. It simply wasn't done in the Wood family.

So when he reached for his leather jacket and pushed her hand from his shoulder, a wry smile twisted his mouth. It was will against will. He was as tall as she was, and much stronger. Whether she liked it or not, she couldn't stop him.

"I told you to go to bed." Her angry black eyes met his stubborn ones.

"And I told you I'm not going." He walked past her to move the thermostat higher, and listen, and to push a rug against the threshold to shut out the draught. Then he began to stack the chairs.

"What are you doing?" she asked.

"I'm bringing the bulbs up here. You can take care of the canned things."

"Chip, I know you're trying to help, but you're acting very foolish. Things don't freeze in a minute. Your leg isn't healed, and you're just asking for trouble. We'll get somebody to start the furnace in the morning."

"Who? Who can get through when the roads aren't plowed? Have you heard the plow? I haven't." He snapped on the cellar light and closed the door behind him.

She was right about the leg. His heavy boots pressed on the bandages and the dull ache had already become a stabbing pain. It was hard not to limp; harder still to bear his weight on the ankle as he carried the heavy cartons up the stairs. But the thermometer was dropping steadily; he must keep going.

After four trips he was ready to quit, but at that moment his mother joined him. She had dressed and combed her hair. Without a word, she began packing quart jars of corn into a large basket and carrying them to the kitchen. Chip couldn't stop then; he had to keep going. He was glad when she called the girls to dress by the kitchen fire; gladder still when she called him to breakfast.

This was a storm all right. The radio said no trains or buses were running; the schools were closed; and the

sub-zero temperature would continue with no relief in
sight.

Chip wondered what to do about the furnace. He
knew it was no job for him. The telephone was still
dead. He might get a message to a plumber, or electrician,
by the men on the snowplow, but that meant digging
out to the road again, and waiting and watching. He
decided the important thing was to save the bulbs, and
there was no time to be wasted doing anything else.

Carol helped him, while Dolly helped her mother with
the food, carrying jelly glasses in her little basket. Chip's
work went more slowly when they reached the barrels,
because the bulbs had to be taken out into smaller boxes
and then laid on newpapers on the dining room floor.

At ten o'clock they stopped for a second breakfast.
Then Chip went outdoors to see if the canvas windbreak
was secure. He breathed deep and felt the little hairs
in his nose freeze. Brushing the snow away, he looked
at the thermometer. Two below zero! But it was beautiful—no fences, no walls, no roads; just snow. The lower
branches of the spruces were buried; the upper ones
sagged under their heavy load; the lilacs were drooping
arches that touched the ground.

Chip's mother rapped on the window, and he went in.
The minute he saw her face, he knew something was
wrong.

"Chip," she said, "the water won't run in the bathroom. Do you know what to do?"

That does it, Chip thought. As though they hadn't
troubles enough already. It was as though some great

wrecking machine, like one he'd seen smashing down the walls of an old mill in Courtney, was trying to finish them. Whamo! Something crumbled; then it swung again, and again, beating, breaking, destroying everything it touched. It seemed that this blow would surely knock down all that was left of his courage. He should have left faucets dripping. He should have thought of pipes. . . .

He knew where the shut-offs were, and the faucets to drain the water system, and the petcocks on the heater. He'd helped his father run a hose out the cellar window to drain the water off, but now the windows were buried in snow.

"Oh, Dad, Dad," he whispered through chattering teeth, "what can I do?"

"Can't you thaw the pipe where it's caught?" his mother asked.

"It would only freeze again."

He went outdoors and managed to clear one window. He struggled with the frozen sash. At last he got it open. He drained as much water as would flow, pulled the hose in, and closed the window.

He was so tired he staggered as he walked across the cellar floor, and there were still a dozen barrels of bulbs to be emptied and carried upstairs, and before night he must repair the bulkhead door. But first, he must rest. The pain was no longer confined to his foot and leg; he ached all over, and cold shivers made his teeth chatter unless he kept his jaws closed tight.

He loaded as many bulbs as it would hold into a bushel basket, and went carefully up the stairs, step by step. He had reached the top, when his numb fingers lost their grip on the basket. It slipped; raked his bad leg and struck his ankle; then went end over end down the stairs.

"Chip, what happened?" his mother cried.

"I dropped it," he said, and collapsed on her bed. In a daze he watched her take off his heavy boots and socks, remove the bandages and bathe the injured leg. He took the medicine she gave him without a word. What a helper he'd turned out to be. Now she'd have it all to do.

Later, he heard the snowplow rumbling past; he heard people talking, and one voice was a man's, but who it was or what they were saying he didn't know, or even care as the half-sleep became the full deep sleep of complete exhaustion.

CHAPTER EIGHTEEN

COURTNEY

When Chip woke, the sun was shining. For a minute he thought he was back in the hospital, but he soon saw it was his mother's room. Dolly was sitting beside him, winding a bandage around her doll's leg.

"You've been asleep a long time," she told him. "The snowplow came, and your teacher came, and the telephone is fixed. And Mama called Uncle Frank, and he's going to take us to Courtney. Do you want some cereal? I can get it for you." She laid her doll on the foot of the bed and covered it with a blanket.

"Where's Mom?"

"She and Carol are packing our clothes."

"But we can't leave now. The bulbs we brought upstairs will freeze." Chip sat up and dropped his heavy head on his hands. If it were only over, this making decisions, setting his will against his mother's. For he would

159

not leave. They could go, but he was staying. As he ate the cream of wheat Dolly brought, he tried to decide what to do first.

However, his mother made the decisions. Dolly would go back with Uncle Frank. The rest of them would stay until Sunday when they would close the house and move to Courtney, and she would go to work.

Chip said he would find a job, too.

"You'll go to school," his mother told him. "Don't talk any more about it." The next morning she rode in with Pat's father and spent the whole day looking for a job and an apartment.

"You won't like it," she said wearily when she got home, "but it's the only place I could find that we can afford. One bedroom, living room with a cot for Chip, and a kitchenette. The lavatory is in the hall."

"Where is the apartment?" Chip asked.

"Cary Street."

"Cary Street?" He couldn't believe he had heard it right. He stared at his mother, then at Carol, who was tilting her chin and blinking and swallowing so her tears wouldn't spill over.

Chip knew Cary Street. Its shabby old houses had once been the homes of well-to-do families, but long since had been made into hives of small apartments. The yards were dumping grounds for rubbish. Only colored people lived there. He had known some of them in school, the Cary Street gang, always in trouble.

"Where are you going to work?"

"In the Wash-Rite Laundry. Sixty dollars a week,

overtime if I want. Dolly will stay at Grandma's, but I'm not sponging on my relatives. You two have been brought up right. You know how to behave yourselves, and there's no reason why you should get into trouble, on Cary Street or anywhere." Suddenly she wilted, burying her face in her arms. "Oh dear Lord," she moaned, "I hope I'm doing the right thing."

Chip couldn't stand it. He got up and went outdoors. His mother in such misery, and here he was, limping around, good for nothing.

In spite of his bandaged leg, he went with his mother and Carol on Saturday to scrub the Cary Street rooms from top to bottom. He tacked clean oil cloth on the kitchen counter and shelves, but the battered furniture and lumpy mattresses had to be endured. He hated the place.

On Sunday they closed the Redfield house. Chip's Uncle Frank loaded his car with the preserves and canned vegetables; Mr. Mahler and Pat took the bulbs and stored them in Pat's cellar.

"You did a good job bringing up so many," Mr. Mahler told Chip. "Some Saturday I'll help you take the frozen stuff out and dump it."

"I'll help, too," Pat promised. "Call me any time, and I'll come for you. And when you come back in the spring we'll all pitch in and help."

Chip was grateful, but he had little to say those days, and even less after they moved to Cary Street. Old Stringer darkened his thoughts of school. Athletics were out. He wanted to be alone, and yet he was so lonely

he could hardly stand it. Every afternoon, after school, he looked for work, but no store would hire him because he was not sixteen. He offered to take care of rubbish barrels, to clean up yards. People gave him suspicious looks and curt refusals, and sometimes boys followed him from house to house, snickering when he was turned away.

By Friday night he was ready to quit. On his way home he passed a little store with toys, dishes and statues of Mary and Jesus jammed in together behind a grimy window. A thin, round-shouldered old Negro sat on a broken chair beside the door. Chip decided to make one more try.

"Can I clean your window, Mister?" he asked. "I'm trying to earn some money."

"What say?" The old man leaned forward, pulling at his ear.

Chip shouted his question. Some boys who were passing began to yell, "Hey, Zeke, can we wash your window? We want some money, too." They surrounded him and Chip, who was ready to use his fists, when a big black boy came out of the next doorway.

"What's the matter now?" he bellowed.

They all tried to tell him, but he shut them up. "Who
are you?" he asked Chip.

"Chip Wood."

"What were you doing to old Zeke?"

"To him? Nothing. I'm looking for work. My mother
and my kid sister have got jobs. I want to find something to do. What's wrong with that?" Chip glared at
the whole crowd.

"Nothing's wrong with that. I've seen you going by,
minding your own business. Listen, you kids. Lay off
him. Do you hear? Can't you see he's a cripple?"

Completely discouraged, Chip limped on home. His
mother was working that night. Carol was with Joanie,
taking care of children for their King Street friends. Chip
slapped bologna on a bun and stirred some instant coffee.
He missed his dad. He missed Dolly, but he was too
tired to walk to his grandmother's, and he hated to spend
money for the bus. Finally he went out and telephoned
Pat Moore.

Pat came the next morning. With Mr. Mahler's help,
they cleaned out the cellar. The soggy, mildewed bulbs
made Chip's heart sick. The Redfield printer, seeing cars
in the yard, delivered the catalogues for *WOOD'S
FLOWER FIELDS*. A bill for sixty-six dollars was tucked
under the string.

"Listen, boy," Mr. Mahler said when Chip showed it
to them, "you've had some hard knocks, but the worst
is over. Your leg is healing. Your father is going to get
better. You're young; you're strong. You're going to carry
on. So why go around looking like an old lost hound dog?"

Chip opened up and talked as they sat on the porch in the sun, eating their lunches. He talked about his father. The X-ray showed the knee was healing; he would soon be out of traction and doing exercises. In a month or so he could come home. But what was there for him to come home to? It would be a long time before he could work. How could they swing it? No car; no money. Chip poured out his questions and his fears. They listened, and talked, and helped him.

"You two ought to be psychiatrists," he concluded with a sour grin. "You ought to lay me on a couch to tell my troubles."

"Everybody has troubles," Mr. Mahler said."The only difference is whether you coddle them or conquer them. Quit feeling sorry for yourself. Get a job. Try a different part of town." He thumped Chip on the back and looked at his watch. "Say, we've sat here an hour. It's time we got busy."

They accomplished a lot that day. "Before we go, I want to show you my room in the barn," Chip said, as they put the wheelbarrows and tools back in the shed and locked up. "This summer I'm going to paint it and make some furniture." He fitted his key into the padlock and rolled back the barn door.

"Wow! Where did that come from?" he exclaimed.

"Why? Isn't it yours?" Pat asked, as Chip stared at the ship on the floor at his feet.

"No. It's Mr. Tower's." Chip told them the story.

"You know this is worth real money," Mr. Mahler said, examining it closely. "It's a beautiful job. There

aren't many of these left, and there aren't many crafts-
men with the know-how and the patience to make them.
Look at that rigging, those shrouds, all brass wire. Chip,
who could have put it in your barn?"

Chip shook his head. "I'm sure I don't know. How
could anybody get in? I suppose we might as well leave
it here until Mr. Tower gets back from Florida, but I
can't understand it." His secret room seemed unimportant
after that discovery.

All the way back to Courtney he kept thinking about
it, and that night, after telling his mother and seeing
her alarm, he lay awake a long time. How could anyone
get into their barn? And even if they could, why should
they leave Mr. Tower's weathervane there? Who would
do a thing like that, and why? Chip wished he had
looked for fingerprints. Too late now, because they had
all handled the ship. As usual, his bright ideas came too
late.

Monday after school, and again Tuesday, he tramped
one street after another. Nobody wanted a car washed,
or any jobs done.

"Oh, what's the use," he said. He spent his last quarter
for a mystery magazine, went home to the empty house,
rested his leg on a chair and began to read.

An hour later, restless and disgusted with himself
he went out into the yard. It was full of battered trash
barrels, old boards and boxes. In one corner was a rusty
bedspring, standing on its side, an old camp cot, some
ragged, soggy blankets and a box of tin cans. That stuff
could be piled up for the city collector to cart away,

Chip decided. At least he could tidy up his own yard.

As he pulled the bedspring over, a spindly-legged little girl came running from the cellar, screaming and throwing things.

"Hey, cut that out," he said, as an old shoe missed his ear by an inch.

"Leave our house alone. Maaa!" she yelled, "the new boy's busting up our house."

A window flew open, and an angry mother called, "What you think you're doing? Leave the kids' playthings alone."

"If I clean up the yard, they'll have a better place to play."

"Mind your business. The yard's all right the way it is. If it ain't good enough for you, go back where you came from."

"Okay. Okay." Chip yanked the springs up again and threw the dirty blanket on top. As he went in to wash his hands, his flash of anger burned out. This was Cary Street. He felt sorry for the little girl and her mother. Hadn't he been ready to quit himself, to sit down and stop trying?

While he lathered his arms, and ran cold water to rinse off the soap, he thought how lucky he'd been to have the parents he had. How lucky to have been born on King Street. And it came to him, as clearly as though a voice spoke the words: That's why you've got to stay with it, and amount to something. You've got to climb the ladder yourself, and help other people, if you can.

Well, while he felt that way, he'd better do something about it. He reached for his English grammar, and went to work on ten sentences using semicolons. That might just possibly hypnotize old Stringer into giving him a passing mark.

He was still at it when his mother came home.

"Mr. Tower came to see me today," she said.

"He's back? Did you tell him about the weathervane?"

"No, I forgot." She took a cup and saucer from the shelf and a pan from its hook.

"When did he get home? What did he want?"

"He got home yesterday. He has a client who wants to buy the farm."

"Our farm?"

She nodded. "He'll pay six thousand."

"Six thousand!" Chip exploded. "Only six thousand after we paid eight, and all we did to the house?" He looked at his mother as she lighted the gas burner. "You told him No, didn't you? Didn't you, Mom?"

"We can't say No, Chip. How can we run a farm? Please don't argue. I gave him the keys. I'm too tired to care."

"Sit down. I'll make your tea."

His eyes blurred as he looked at the dirty windows and dangling venetian blinds of the house next door. He was seeing fields of flowers and a brook running over white stones, pines and spruces and a holly tree on a snowy hill. He was seeing a little red house with sunshine streaming through the windows, firelight flickering on a wall, and his family there, his mother knitting, Carol with her books, Dolly coloring pictures, and his dad reading the paper in the big chair the office had given him.

"They ought to pay as much as we did," he said, as he put the tea pot and some cookies on the table.

"They won't. Mr. Tower put it plainly. No white person wants to live where Negroes have lived."

The room was very quiet as she sipped her tea.

"Did he say anything about the accident?"

A slow flush crept up her neck and tinged her ears with pink. "He feels no responsibility whatever, because we have known from the beginning that he did not want Sharon to . . . to associate with us." The words had been burned into her memory, Chip could see, never to be forgotten. "He said he had been broadminded about her befriending us, but your father had no business going to meet her."

"What did you say?"

Her ears grew pinker. "I . . . I can't remember. I'm afraid I lost my head. Let's not talk about it."

The next day Chip went to school with several things besides lessons on his mind. At lunch, Joanie and Carol were eating with him and Butch. Every time Chip saw Joanie, he felt a new surprise. All of a sudden she had changed from a rowdy little girl to a very pretty little big girl.

They were talking about jobs when she said, "Why don't you try Davis' greenhouse? He knows your dad, and you're good with plants. You could come to my house for supper, if you wanted to." Her brown eyes dropped shyly.

"I'll go to see him. Right away. And thanks for the invite." Chip looked at her long lashes and cute little mouth. Watch it, boy, he said to himself. Don't get off the beam. It's a job you want, not a girl friend . . . not yet, anyway.

Carol loaned him a quarter for bus fare, and Chip rode across town after school. Mr. Davis, a kindly old Scotchman, had bought pansy plants from the Woods for years, and Chip had often wandered through his three small greenhouses. It would be the perfect job, if he could only get it. And he'd be learning. He just had to get it. By the time he arrived, he was so nervous he could hardly speak, but Mr. Davis hired him.

"Sure, Chip," he said, "you'll be my apprentice, and if it's greenhouses you want to learn about, I'll teach you all there is to know."

Chip, beaming from ear to ear, listened and worked, and could hardly be persuaded to go home for supper.

CHAPTER NINETEEN

STARS

From that day on, his job in the greenhouse was all that Chip could talk about. On Friday night he brought home his first pay.

"Everything's going to be all right now, Mom," he told her, as she washed her hair at the kitchen sink. "And look at this." He waved a paper in front of her face.

"What is it? I can't see."

"It's an A on that English paper. The first A Stringer ever gave me."

"Are you going to frame it?"

"No, I want you to show it to Dad, when you go Sunday."

"I had a letter today. He's out of traction and up in a wheel chair. Isn't that wonderful? With the massage and physiotherapy he'll soon be walking."

"I knew it, Mom." Chip's grin spread from ear to ear. "Didn't I tell you? Didn't I say he'd get better?"

"Yes. I remember. Thank God you were right."

"Sure I was right. Wow! Three good things in one week! You know how Grandma's always talking about luck coming with the stars, Pluto in Leo or something? I think it's true."

"Nonsense. There's not a word of truth in it."

"Well, something's changed. We had bad luck for weeks and weeks, and now I've got a job; Dad's better; everything's O.K."

"Is that someone knocking?" She wrapped her head in a towel as Chip opened the door. Mr. Collins stood there, with a stout, red-faced man.

"How d'you do. This is my son, Leonard."

They all shook hands, Mrs. Wood embarrassed by her towel turban, Chip fearing disaster as the younger Mr. Collins insisted that Mrs. Wood sit in the only sturdy chair while he sank into the creaking depths of the cot bed, beside Chip. They had been to see Inga, they said, and she had told them about the accident.

"How is your husband getting along?" Mr. Collins asked.

"Very nicely." Mrs. Wood read them parts of the letter with its good news.

"Fine! Fine! Well, we came on business, and we'd better get to it. Leonard and his wife go to Cape Cod every summer. They either get a housekeeper to look after me, or I go to one of those nursing homes. I'm sick of 'em, and I wonder if you'd take me as a boarder when

you go back to Redfield. I wouldn't be a mite of trouble.
I could ramble around, and pull a few weeds if I felt
like it, or sit on the porch in the sun."

Chip waited for his mother to speak. She opened her
mouth and closed it. He hoped she wasn't going to cry.

"I said I'd never go back to the old place," Mr. Collins
went on. "Afraid it would make me homesick. But now
I want to go so bad I can hardly wait to get there."

"We've decided it would do him good," his son agreed.

"I wish I could say Yes," Mrs. Wood began, "but . . .
but I'm afraid we won't be there ourselves. Mr. Tower
has a client who wants to buy it."

"The devil he does," Mr. Collins burst out. "Don't
let him have it."

"That's what I said. He's only offering six thousand,"
Chip told them.

"What? Only six thousand, when you paid eight, and
put in plumbing?" Leonard Collins leaned forward suddenly and the bed springs groaned. "I can't understand
that. J.P.'s always been out for all the commission he
can get."

"It's because we're colored," Mrs. Wood explained.

"Mr. Collins, did you ever try to sell it for five thousand? Somebody told me you did." Chip's face burned
as they all stared at him in surprise.

"Yes, the land and barn, after my wife died; not the
house. Why?"

"They said you . . . you raised the price, but I didn't
believe it. Not after I met you."

"I'm glad of that. Now let's get back to business.

You're not going to sell the farm. I pay ten dollars a day at the nursing home for a room where there ain't space to swing a cat by the tail. I'd a sight rather pay that money to you, and it would tide you over until your husband gets back on his feet."

Chip whooped. "Mom, we could get along on that. Pat says he'll help me this summer, and I can take care of a small garden. Can I call Mr. Tower and tell him and his client to go jump in the brook?"

"Why don't we ride out and tell him?" Mr. Collins chuckled as his son struggled up from his low seat.

"I have things to do here, but Chip can go," Mrs. Wood said. "And the minute you see Mr. Tower, tell him about the weathervane."

"What weathervane's that?" Mr. Collins asked.

"The one that used to be on our barn. The one you gave to Mr. Tower," Chip told them.

"What?" Mr. Collins shouted.

His son looked at the old man in astonishment. "Father, you didn't give our ship to Jud Tower?"

"Of course I didn't. I'd have chopped it up for kindling first. It was given to me by the man who made it, an old sea captain. Did you ever notice how perfectly it's balanced? That's because two thirds of the ship is aft of the rod . . ." He ran out off breath and had to stop.

"Yes, Father, but what did you tell Jud?" his son asked.

"I told him No. He wanted to buy, but I told him it wasn't for sale. It had been on that barn for nigh onto forty years, and it was going to stay there. Who took it off? Where is it now?"

"It's in our barn, the ship part," Chip began. Then, seeing their bewilderment, he went back to the beginning of the story, telling how it was there on the cupola on Saturday when they went to look at the farm, and gone on the following Thursday, and then last December stolen from Mr. Tower's garage.

"He accused Chip of stealing it," his mother broke in. "And now he must have seen it when he showed the clients around, and he'll be sure to make trouble."

The younger Mr. Collins turned to face Chip. "You say somebody put it in your barn?"

"Yes sir. I found it the day I cleaned out the cellar with Pat Moore and Mr. Mahler. He's my teacher. He helped us."

"Who do you think might have done it?"

Chip shook his head. "I don't know. I can't figure out why anybody would do it."

The old man opened the door. "Come on. Let's go see Jud. We'll straighten this business out once and for all. It makes me so thundering mad . . ."

"Be careful what you say," his son warned. "It won't help to lose your temper with J.P."

"Who said I'd lose my temper? I haven't been the father of a smart young lawyer all these years without learning a few things."

They drove directly to Mr. Tower's house, where they found Freddy's blue car and Jud's red convertible parked in the driveway. Chip wondered if Sharon, also, was home for the weekend. She wasn't.

If Mr. Tower was surprised to see them, he did not show it. He greeted the Collinses warmly, asked if they remembered Jud Junior, introduced Freddy Greer, and congratulated the old gentleman on his recovery. Chip, left alone in the background, waved to Inga as she popped her head in the door and then disappeared.

Old Mr. Collins went right to the point. "We came for the keys, Jud. I've been talking to Mrs. Wood, and she has decided not to sell. And what's all this nonsense about the weathervane?" At the mention of the weathervane, it seemed to Chip that everyone in the room became tense and watchful.

Mr. Tower leaned forward, his face solemn, his long hands clasped between his knees. "If you are referring to the old ship weathervane that was on your barn so many years," he said, "I am afraid I have unpleasant news for you." He stopped, cleared his throat, apologized for doing it, and went on. "You remember how surprised and delighted I was when you said I could have it . . ."

"I don't recollect saying anything like that," Mr. Collins declared, his keen eyes never moving from the long, thin face.

"Have you forgotten?" Mr. Tower's voice was so pleasant and patient that for a minute Chip wondered if the old man *had* forgotten.

"My memory's pretty good, but we'll talk about that later—you and me, and Leonard. Now, Chip tells me he found the weathervane in his barn. What's the story?"

Chip, watching the boys on the divan opposite him, saw Freddy pick up a magazine and begin to read, while Jud stared at his father, grinding one cigarette into the ash tray, nervously lighting another. He's worried, Chip thought. I wonder if he knows Mr. Collins didn't give the ship to his father . . . what could be worse than that . . . to know your father would steal . . . and lie. . . .

But Mr. Tower was talking again, and looking at Chip. "It was stolen from my garage last December. Now, I am not accusing Chip of stealing it, but the fact remains that I know he admired the ship and wanted it. I have observed him on several occasions looking at it carefully. Of course I do not know what he was thinking, or planning to do. But since I took clients to the Wood's farm, and found it in his barn, I am forced by the unquestionable though most regrettable evidence to conclude that he took it."

"Is that the only conclusion you could come to?" the younger Mr. Collins asked.

"What other? Has he told you how it came to be there?"

"He doesn't know how it got there," the old man interrupted.

"My dear old friend, isn't it a strange coincidence . . ."

"No," Mr. Collins roared. "Chip doesn't lie. He doesn't steal. I'm going to tell you how I know." He took a deep breath. "He found my old stamp book in the desk in the barn. He collects stamps so he knew these were valuable. And his family needed money. But what does he do? He brings them to me. Hands them over to the housekeeper. Not looking for any reward, just doing the honest thing because that's the way he's been brought up."

Mr. Tower's face was like a mask as he listened, but Chip could see the muscles of his jaw tighten and relax and tighten again as he clenched his teeth. "I am sorry if I misjudged the boy," he said at last.

"I'd say you'd misjudged the whole family. They're fine people, Jud, fine, honest, hard-working people. And they're kind. They're taking me to board this summer."

"Oh? We'll all welcome your return."

"But it won't seem like home without the weathervane. Suppose you let it stay where it is until we have our little talk. What do you say, Jud?"

"I'll do more than that. So that there may be no unpleasantness between old friends, I'll see that it is put back on the barn." Taking the key ring from his pocket, he slipped the barn key off and passed the others to Chip. "I'll return this to your mother when the vane is replaced."

"Thank you," Chip said.

Mr. Collins poked him with his finger. "You want to say anything before we go?"

"Yes. I'd like to know who put it in my barn."

"It was somebody who had a grudge against you."

Chip's skin prickled. Somehow, although he had no proof, he'd always suspected Freddy, and seeing his old enemy so much at home in the Tower house made him sure he was right. "I think Freddy put it there. He tried to chop down the holly tree to get my goat, and when

I stopped him he said he'd get even." Chip leaned forward, his eyes blazing. "You did it, didn't you, to make it look as though I stole it."

Freddy closed the magazine and gave Chip an insolent stare.

"You could get into trouble saying things like that," he warned. "I have never even seen the weathervane. And I did not try to chop down your holly tree."

"Holly tree? What's the holly tree got to do with it?" Mr. Collins demanded. "How did he know there was a holly tree?"

"Sharon told him."

For a minute the only sound was the old man's wheezy breathing. Then Inga Paulson walked into the room.

"Sharon did not tell him," she said.

"Inga!" The word burst out before Mr. Tower could stop it. "We have guests."

"Ya. I know. I been listening. But I'm not staying behind the door while Sharon gets blamed for something she didn't do. Jud tried to make her tell, and when she wouldn't he went up on the hill and watched with field glasses . . ."

"Binoculars, Inga," Jud interrupted, a sneer on his face as he looked first at Freddy and then at his father. "It was an initiation stunt. Freddy was told to bring in the holly . . ." he stopped to light another cigarette, then went on, "and the weathervane. He was supposed to put it back, but there was snow on the ground and footprints would show. Chip's family had left for Courtney, so we put it in his barn." He jerked a thumb at his father. "We already had the keys J.P. keeps in his desk."

The silence that followed was like the moment of quiet between a flash of lightning and the expected thunder. No one moved. Mr. Collins may have stopped breathing for he made no sound. Freddy's face was scarlet. Inga stood like a statue in the middle of the floor.

A slow flush crept up Mr. Tower's neck and his eyes burned with anger as he looked at his son. "I had forgotten there was a second set of keys. Get them. Give them to Chip."

"Have you still got them, Freddy?" Jud drawled. "We intended to put the old thing back on the garage before you got home from Florida." He took the keys from his fraternity brother and threw them to Chip.

"If you had shared your little secrets with me it would have saved us a great deal of trouble." The sarcasm in Mr. Tower's quiet voice cut like a knife.

"At least I told the truth," Jud blurted out, "and that's more than you did tonight. Mr. Collins never gave you the weathervane. He knows it, and you know it, and so do I. You talk about other people stealing and lying..."

Mr. Tower sprang to his feet. "You'll regret this outburst, this unpardonable rudeness..."

Young Jud slammed past him toward the door. "Oh what's the use? I'm getting out...leaving...and this time I'm not coming back." He flung open the door and went out into the night, Freddy following at his heels. First one, then the other car roared down the driveway.

"I'm sorry, Jud," Mr. Collins said. "I tried to make it easy for you because I didn't want to shame you in front of your boy and his friend. But it was too late. And the worst of it is you have only yourself to blame. Well, Leonard, Chip, we've got the keys and we've found out what we wanted to know. Let's go home."

Later that night, after he had told his mother all that happened, Chip concluded, "So we get our weathervane back. Now what do you say about lucky stars?"

"You're a star," she said, and for the first time in months he saw the dimple in her cheek.

CHAPTER TWENTY

REUNION

During the next two weeks Chip's time was taken up by the greenhouse, where the benches were filled with lilies, tulips and daffodils for the Easter trade. He sifted potting soil, made cuttings, transplanted geraniums, ran errands, waited on customers, and in his spare time planted seed flats for his own garden. He worked hard and happily.

Once a week he had supper at Joanie's, and another night at his grandmother's where Dolly flung herself into his arms and strangled him with her hugs.

"Daddy's got fizzy-gull therapies," she screamed in his ear. "He can bend his knee, and he's coming home in two weeks." And then it was one week, and then tomorrow.

Joanie's brother, home on leave, took Mrs. Wood to Boston to get her husband. It was decided he should

182

stay at Grandmother's until the Redfield house was ready.

It was wonderful to see him again. He looked well, relaxed and cheerful. He showed them how he could walk with a cane, and he showed them the knee case and leg brace which he would have to wear for a while. He described the exercises he had to do. Everybody talked at once, except Chip, who found himself strangely tongue-tied, listening to the others, but seeing only his father. It was too great a happiness to be noisy about.

They were to go back to the farm during April vacation. Easter would be over, and the greenhouse rush would slacken off. Mrs. Wood had already given her notice at the laundry. On Monday they would ride out to see about getting a man to help Chip with the gardens, and have a plumber come to see about repairs to the water pipes.

Since it was going to be a real occasion, Chip telephoned Mr. Mahler and Pat to come for them, in both cars, so that Joanie and Butch and Mr. Collins could go with them for the day. Then, later in the week, the Woods and Mr. Collins would go to stay.

Vacation came at last. Sunday was a busy day, with the women getting ready for Monday, packing things, and getting lunches ready to take. Chip had his first chance for a good talk with his father, a long, serious talk.

It reminded Chip of the April day, just a year ago, when they had talked in the potting shed. How sure he'd been then that everything would turn out right. He knew better now. He knew hard times lay ahead. He had passed forever that foolish optimism that says try hard and everything will be wonderful. It won't. But you have to keep on trying.

"It'll take time, Dad," he said, "but we're going to have that greenhouse. And I'm going to Mass. State and take up horticulture. I'll work for scholarships. I know now what I want to do."

"Whatever else this winter did," his father said, "I can see it was good for you."

"Maybe. But one's enough."

The next morning the Woods and Joanie and Butch were on the porch of Grandmother's house at eight sharp. A few minutes later Mr. Collins came in a taxi. They waited ten minutes, fifteen, talking happily, but neither Mr. Mahler nor Pat showed up. Chip began to get anxious. It seemed funny that neither one was on time.

When they arrived, half an hour late, they were both in Mr. Mahler's Ford. Raspberries, Chip thought, that does it. The Woods can squeeze in, but not Mr. Collins, or Butch or Joanie. Maybe he had a hole in his head where his brains ought to be, but he'd been counting on Joanie's going.

"Where's your car, Pat?" he called.

"I didn't bring it," he said, trying to hide a grin.

Chip couldn't see anything to smile about.

"Carol, you and Dolly will have to stay with Joanie," Mrs. Wood said. "Maybe her father will bring you out later. Butch, you'll have to wait until the next time we go."

"I think we all ought to go," Mr. Collins declared. "What's the matter with that blue car across the street?

Looks like we could all get in there without crowding."

They all looked at the shiny blue station wagon on the other side of the street. Then they looked at Mr. Collins, who was fishing through his pockets for something.

"Oh. Here they are!" He took out two keys on a ring and gave them to Pat. "You like to drive, young feller? See if these keys are any good."

Pat crossed the street and they all trailed after him. He unlocked the door and started the motor. "Boy, that's sweet, Mr. Collins," he said, cocking an ear to listen to the quiet hum.

"Whose car is it?" Chip asked. "Is it yours, Pat? Is it Mr. Collins'?" A smile spread over his face. That would be something, if Mr. Collins had bought a car.

"Well," the old man said, "I couldn't figure out how we could get along without a car. Maybe I'd ought to have waited and asked Chip first, but I didn't. I sold those stamps and bought this station wagon, or rather my son did. It's not new, but it's only gone twenty thousand miles, and he says it's as good as new. Pat will drive us out, and Mr. Wood will drive us home."

Nobody said anything. They couldn't for a minute. Dolly squatted down to look at her reflection in the shiny hub cap.

"Gee, thanks," Chip said huskily, and then everybody thanked him.

"Don't thank me, thank Chip. Open the tailboard, boy; show them all the room you got." As delighted as a grandfather playing Santa Claus, he had them looking into the back, and into the motor, and pushing buttons and playing the radio.

"I guess I'll have to drive back alone," Mr. Mahler said, when there was nothing more to be seen.

Dolly and Mr. Collins were already in the new car, with no intention of leaving. "Joanie, why don't we ride back with Mr. Mahler?" Chip asked. "We can ride in the new car some other day."

"All right," and deserting Carol, Joanie slid in with Chip. No April morning had ever seemed so beautiful, no birds' songs had ever been so gay, no April breeze so sweet, no miles as short as those between Courtney and Redfield.

"Our weathervane's back," Chip shouted as they came within sight of the barn. His mouth hung open, for there were cars in the yard; someone with brown horses was plowing the dahlia fields; boys and girls with rakes and wheelbarrows were clearing away the winter rubble and piling it to burn.

"What . . . what's going on?" Chip asked.

"Get out and see," Mr. Mahler said. "Pat started it, and it ran away with him. You folks have a lot of friends in Redfield."

It was true. Chip knew it; so did his father and mother and the girls when they got out and looked around.

Friends. Good friends. It was Quint Brown plowing; it was his sister Merlene, now in Carol's arms, who was taking care of the Hayden children while their mother washed the windows on the porch. Boys and girls they knew in school were pushing the wheel barrows. They

came crowding around to thump Chip on the back, and
to ask Mr. Wood how he was getting along, all talking
at once, admiring the car, being introduced to Mr. Collins, and Butch and Joanie.

Only one girl kept on weeding, pulling grass and
runaway-robin from among the lilies of the valley. Chip
hesitated a minute, then went to her. "Hello, Sharon,"
he said, "come on over and see my father."

She shook her head without looking up. "No. I only
came to help until you got here because I know more
about the garden than they do. I'm going now." She
stood up and wiped her hands on her dungarees.

"You can't go without speaking to my dad and the
girls."

"They don't want to see me." She turned her face
away, but not before Chip saw tears glistening in her
eyes. "It doesn't do any good to say it now, but tell
them I'm . . . I'm sorry." She started across the yard like
a lonely shadow on the bright day. It didn't seem right
to let her go like that.

"Dolly," Chip called, "there's Sharon. Catch her, and
tell her to come back."

"Sharon," Dolly shrieked.

"Sharon," Carol echoed, running after Dolly. They
caught Sharon and tried to persuade her to come back
with them.

Chip saw his father whispering to his mother. She
shook her head at first, and then, as he kept on talking
to her, she nodded. As Sharon pulled away from the
girls, Mrs. Wood called, "Sharon . . . we want to see you,"

and held out her arms. In another minute, Sharon was in them, crying wildly. Mr. Wood patted his wife's shoulder and smiled.

Mr. Collins, who was enjoying it all, walked over to Chip and Joanie.

"I'll be jiggered if I can understand women," he said. "When they're happy, they cry. When they aren't happy, they cry. I never could figure out where they get all them tears."

Joanie giggled her cute little giggle. Chip grinned and passed her a rake. "Get with it, kid," he said, and whistling like a canary, he went to join the boys.